MILLS
Centenary Collection

**Celebrating 100 years of romance with
the very best of Mills & Boon**

*First published in Great Britain 2008
by Harlequin Mills & Boon Limited,
Eton House, 18-24 Paradise Road, Richmond, Surrey TW9 1SR*

© Liz Fielding 2004

ISBN: 978 0 263 86642 1

76-0708

Harlequin Mills & Boon policy is to use papers that are natural, renewable and recyclable products and made from wood grown in sustainable forests. The logging and manufacturing processes conform to the legal environmental regulations of the country of origin.

*Printed and bound in Spain
by Litografia Rosés S.A., Barcelona*

The Temp and
the Tycoon

by
Liz Fielding

◉™ MILLS & BOON®
Pure reading pleasure

Liz Fielding was born with itchy feet. She made it to Zambia before her twenty-first birthday and, gathering her own special hero and a couple of children on the way, lived in Botswana, Kenya and Bahrain – with pauses for sightseeing pretty much everywhere in between. She finally came to a full stop in a tiny Welsh village cradled by misty hills and these days, mostly, leaves her pen to do the travelling. When she's not sorting out the lives and loves of her characters, she potters in the garden, reads her favourite authors and spends a lot of time wondering… "What if…"

For news of upcoming books – and to sign up for her occasional newsletter – visit Liz's website at www.lizfielding.com

CHAPTER ONE

'WAIT for me!'

Talie Calhoun sprinted across the marble lobby of the Radcliffe Tower as the lift doors began to close. The occupant of the lift obliged by holding the doors, and she beamed a grateful smile in his direction.

'Thank you so much! It's my first day and I am sooo late,' she said, all in a rush as she checked her wristwatch and let out a tiny wail of anguish before looking up at her fellow passenger. Nothing unusual there. Looking up was what she did, mostly. Her grandmother had warned her. If she didn't eat up her spinach and crusts she wouldn't grow tall and her hair wouldn't curl.

One out of two to granny.

Oh, good grief. It was just her luck that the man was a serious babe magnet. Slate grey eyes, cheekbones to die for, a mouth that you just knew would melt your bones. If you were in the market to have your bones melted, that was. In short, the kind of man that you wouldn't want to meet unless your make-up was perfect, your clothes elegant—but sexy—and your hair totally in control. Instead, she was pink in the face, dishevelled and flustered. She wasn't even going to think about her hair…

'That's not good, is it?' she said, offering a smile. But if she'd been hoping for reassurance, she was out of luck.

'It does suggest a certain lack of enthusiasm,' he replied coolly.

Would it have hurt the wretch to smile?

'Which floor?' he enquired.

'Oh…' She consulted the card she was holding. 'Thirty-two, please.' Then, as her knight errant pressed the button for her floor, 'It's not true, you know,' she said. 'I am *incredibly* enthusiastic.'

He lifted his left eyebrow no more than a millimetre. It expressed a world-weary lack of belief that she found totally galling.

'No, honestly!' she protested. Then, 'But you're probably right. This may be the shortest temp job in the entire history of temping.'

'If it was important, maybe you should have set your alarm a little earlier.' Her outraged response to this calumny was still a fledgling thought when he said, 'Who are you going to work for?'

'The Finance Director.'

'Then you *are* in trouble.'

A twinge of unease tightened her stomach. She couldn't be that unlucky…

'Look, it wasn't my fault. My alarm was set for six o'clock. I was *almost* here an hour ago.'

'I should perhaps warn you that the Finance Director never accepts "almost" as good enough.'

'Please… Tell me that you're not him…'

'No. You're safe for another couple of minutes.' His smile was definitely worth waiting for. Tiny creases appeared at the corners of his mouth and eyes to demonstrate that, although it was more ironic than ha-ha-ha, it was the genuine article.

'Whew!' she said, flapping her hand as if to cool her cheeks— actually, it wasn't wholly pretence. 'That would have been a really bad start.'

'Late is bad enough. Have you got a good excuse prepared? Delay on the Underground is a favourite, I believe.'

'With good reason,' she declared. 'But it wasn't anything that simple. I wish it was.'

The eyebrow did its job again, inviting her to elaborate. Or maybe in disbelief… 'Look, it's just me, okay? I seem to have this fatal attraction for calamity, mayhem and misadventure. Today it was some poor man having a seizure down in the Underground.'

'That's a reason for him being late, not you,' he pointed out.

'Yes, but I will get *involved*.'

'Oh. I see.'

For a moment she suspected that he was laughing at her. No, his mouth was perfectly straight…

She dragged her gaze from the kind of lower lip that sent a rush of hormones to her brain.

'He'd, um, collapsed on the platform. People were walking right past him. I suppose they thought he'd been taking drugs or something. It wasn't exactly a rerun of *While You Were Sleeping*—'

'I'm sorry?'

'The movie? Where the girl rescues the guy when he falls onto the track and then everyone thinks she's his fiancée…' She stopped. Clearly he hadn't a clue what she was talking about. 'Obviously I couldn't just leave him there.'

'Obviously,' he said. And then he did smile. Really smile. He was clearly killing himself with the effort not to laugh out loud.

Why did men *always* do that?

Because she was only five foot three in her thickest socks and twenty pounds overweight, according to some stupid height/weight chart in one of her aunt's slimming magazines?

Why was it that only tall, thin people were taken seriously?

'You find that funny?' she demanded.

'No! No, absolutely not,' he said, rapidly losing the smile. 'You weren't afraid?' Then, 'I suspect that's why none of those people stopped.'

'Of course it was, but he was sick. He needed help. I grabbed the nearest person and wouldn't let go until the poor woman got out her mobile phone and called for an ambulance. Then I did what I could to make him comfortable. Of course it took the paramedics forever to get through the rush hour traffic, and then I had to stay and explain what had happened, what I'd done.'

'Is he going to be all right?'

Okay. He'd smiled at the wrong moment, but he had asked the right question…

'I think so. He was a bit dazed, but he seemed to have pretty much recovered by the time I finally got away.' The lift stopped, the doors slid back. 'Uh-oh. This is my floor. Well, thanks for holding the lift.'

'Anytime. Just yell,' he said, and then he smiled again. And her bones…melted.

Oh, good grief. She'd yelled… In the hallowed precincts of the Radcliffe Tower…

'I only do that in an emergency,' she said, again wishing she was six inches taller so that people would take her seriously.

She was tired of men smiling indulgently at her. Not that she could have done anything about it if they were gazing at her with undiluted passion. But even so. A girl needed a morale boost once in a while.

'Keep your fingers crossed for me.'

'I will,' he said, then spoiled the effect by saying, 'But I doubt that will be necessary. I suspect you could talk your way out of anything.'

Jude Radcliffe was still smiling as he walked into his own suite of offices on the top floor of the tower. Catching his PA's startled expression, he straightened his face and said, 'Call Mike Garrett, will you, please, Heather? Tell him I'd appreciate it if he didn't give his temp a hard time about being late. She dealt with a medical emergency on the Underground on her way to work.'

'Good heavens. Was it serious?' Then, with a frown, 'What were you doing on the Underground?'

'I suspect it was dramatic, rather than life-threatening, and I wasn't involved. I just rode up in the lift with the woman.'

'You seem to have covered a lot of ground in a short time. What's her name?' she asked, picking up the telephone.

'She never stopped talking long enough for me to ask her.'

'Obviously she had no idea who you were.'

'I doubt that it would have made any difference.'

'Really? Well, good for her. Description?'

'How many temps do you think they'll have arriving late in Finance?' he said, suddenly regretting the impulse to get involved. 'She's small, with hair like an exploding mattress.'

'What colour mattress?'

'Blonde.'

'Ah.'

Ah? What did 'ah' mean? He refused to ask.

'Keep an eye on her, will you? See how she does. If we've got a suitable permanent opening we might consider her. If she's interested.' Realising that Heather was looking at him with a speculative little smile, he said, 'The woman stopped to help a total stranger when everyone else walked by. People like that are rare.'

'If she was telling the truth. It must have occurred to you that she might simply have been lying in wait for you to arrive with this heart-touching story well prepared?'

That he hadn't—not for one minute—was disturbing. It was usually his first thought, and his last one, too. 'Anything is possible,' he replied, and, in an attempt to discourage any foolish ideas that might be lingering in Heather's normally intelligent head, 'Which is the reason I asked you to keep an eye on her.'

'Right. Of course it is. And which is most important, Jude? Her skills or her social conscience?'

At which point he knew that he was being teased. That his PA thought he'd been snagged by some eye candy with an above average IQ who'd taken the trouble to use more than her looks as bait. And that, for once in a long while, he'd fallen for it.

'You've been working for me too long to ask that,' he said, deciding that enough was enough. 'When you've spoken to Mike, bring in the New York file. I want to fine-tune the details before I leave for Scotland.'

Talie enjoyed working for the Radcliffe Group. The job was demanding, but she relished the opportunity to stretch herself. So much of her time in the last couple of years had been lived within the confines of her home; the chance to get out into the workplace, talk to some people who knew nothing about her, do ordinary stuff for a couple of weeks, was her version of respite.

Even if it meant having to cope with her aunt's attempts to get her involved in a slimming regime.

Her only disappointment was that she hadn't met her knight errant of the lift again. She'd hoped to thank him properly. She would put him right about Mike Garrett, too. Mike had been *totally* understanding about why she was late that first morning, was an absolute sweetheart to work for, and she sincerely wished she had more than just the one week standing in as holiday cover for his secretary.

Unlike the eponymous owner of the Tower.

Jude Radcliffe, according to her new colleagues, who'd whisked her off to their favourite lunchtime watering hole and wasted no time at all in filling her in on just how lucky she was not to have been assigned to the top floor, was a total bastard to work for.

She might have dismissed this as pique that their personal billionaire, although apparently sex-on-legs and unaccountably unattached, was totally oblivious to their charms. However, a couple of the other senior secretaries who'd worked for him when his PA was away shuddered so convincingly at the memory that she knew it had to be true.

His PA was considered to be something of a dragon, too, although she'd seemed pleasant enough when she'd stopped at Talie's desk later in the week to ask if Mike was free, taking the time to ask how Talie was settling in, make sure she'd found her way around, ask what her plans were, suggest she leave her CV with Human Resources.

Since Jude was away the week she worked for his company she didn't have the opportunity to check him out for herself. Apparently his idea of a holiday was walking in the Scottish Highlands—shock, horror, face-pulling all around. It didn't sound that terrible to Talie, but she didn't say so. She was a temp, and her opinion didn't count. She was just there to listen. But it was clear the rest of his employees felt the least he could do was indulge himself in a lavish lifestyle and give them something to gossip about over the skinny latte. And when they looked at her, expecting her to agree that the man was a disappointment all around, she did her best to hide her amusement and agreed with them.

'Natalie! I can hear the phone!'

She was already halfway down the stairs before her mother called out. Phone calls early in the morning or late at night always meant bad news and she snatched it up. 'Yes?'

'Talie? Talie Calhoun? This is Heather Lester. From the Radcliffe Group? We spoke—'

'I remember,' she said. 'I'm sorry if I snapped, but I was—'

'Asleep. I'm the one who should apologise, for disturbing you in the middle of the night. I do know how unsettling late-night phone calls can be. Unfortunately I've got a bit of a crisis and it wouldn't wait until morning.'

About to explain that she hadn't been asleep, Talie said, 'Oh.' Then, 'What kind of crisis?'

'Before I go into details, can I just ask if you have a valid passport?'

'Well, yes.' She had once had a life and holidays abroad, like ordinary people.

'Well, that's the first hurdle. The thing is, I'm supposed to be flying to New York with Mr Radcliffe tomorrow morning—actually, it's this morning now—but my daughter has gone into labour two weeks early and her husband is away, so she needs me.'

'And you need someone to take your place?'

'At zero notice.'

'And you're asking me?' Talie caught her breath. 'To go to New York?' With the total bastard?

'My choice is limited. There aren't too many secretaries who can take shorthand verbatim. And Mike spoke very highly of you.'

'He did? Gosh, how kind of him. I'd give him a reference as a great boss anytime.'

'That speaks volumes in itself. He'd rather type his own reports than cope with incompetence. However, I'd be lying if I said he was as difficult as Jude. I wouldn't want you to get the impression that this trip will be a holiday. It'll be damned hard work.'

Yes, but it would be damned hard work in New York!

She hugged the excitement close to her chest and said, 'Well, of course. I don't imagine Mr Radcliffe takes his secretary away with him purely for decoration,' she said. And then clapped her hand over her mouth as she realised how that must sound. 'Oh, crumbs. I didn't mean—'

'It's okay, Talie. I know exactly what you meant. The other thing I have to impress on you is the need for total discretion.'

'I always assumed that was the first requirement of the job, Mrs Lester. But if you're concerned, then maybe you should send someone you know.'

'It's Heather. And I'm asking you. Yes or no? Will you go?'

Reality beckoned.

'I'd absolutely love to, but the thing is I've already got another temp job lined up and I can't let them down—'

'I've already spoken to the agency. They will rearrange the booking if you are willing to take this assignment.'

In the middle of the night?

Apparently sensing her disbelief, Heather said, 'I'm a personal friend of the manager. Who speaks very highly of you, I might add.'

'Oh, I see. Well, if you're sure. I mean, surely there's someone else at the office…' She stopped, remembering how the other women at the office spoke about Jude Radcliffe. 'Who can do shorthand,' she finally managed.

Heather laughed. 'Not like you, Talie. You'll have my undying gratitude if you'll take this on.'

And clearly the undying gratitude of the right-hand woman to Jude Radcliffe was something well worth having. In the unlikely event that she would ever be able to take on a full time job.

Assuming that all objections were disposed of, Heather went on, 'A car will pick you up at nine-thirty to take you to the airport. The driver will have everything you need in a carry-on bag, including some notes I made in case something like this happened.'

'Heavens, that was lucky.'

'Not lucky. It's called forward planning. Babies have a habit of doing their own thing. You'll have my laptop, too, and there's everything you'll need on that. Jude's been away, so I'm sure he'll want to work on the plane. Have you got a notebook handy?'

Heather spent ten minutes or so briefing her before rushing back to her daughter. Talie replaced the receiver and sat on the bottom of the stairs for a moment, staring down at the pages of shorthand notes she'd taken down, utterly stupefied by the speed at which events had overtaken her.

She needed to move. She needed to pack…

'Who was that?' Her mother's voice finally filtered through the disbelief that something so amazing could have happened to her. 'Who could be so thoughtless, calling at this time of night?'

She stirred, went back upstairs to her mother's room. 'It's okay, Mum, it was work. A special temping job has come up and I'm going to have to go away for a few days—'

'Away? Where? I can't—'

'You'll be fine,' she said, firmly putting a stop to her mother's panicky reaction. 'Karen is here until the end of the month, remember? And I'll ring you every day.' She decided it would be wiser not to mention exactly where she'd be phoning from… 'I bought some videos for you today,' she said, changing the subject. 'A couple of old Doris Day movies.'

'Really?' Her mother brightened momentarily. Then, 'If only your father were here.'

'I know, Mum. I know.' She brushed the hair back from her mother's forehead and kissed her. 'You go back to sleep. I'll bring you some breakfast before I leave tomorrow.'

'Heather? I've been trying to get you all morning. What's this damn nonsense about you not coming to New York? I'm at the airport and the flight has already been called.'

'I'm sorry, Jude. I did try and get you last night, but I could only get your answering machine and it ran out before I could explain—'

'And then you switched off your phone.'

'I can't have it on in the hospital.'

'Hospital! What hospital? What's happened?'

'Nothing to worry about. It's just my daughter. She's gone into labour early and she's having a bit of a torrid time, poor darling. They're considering a Caesar—'

'And you're a surgeon?' He didn't wait for an answer. 'Stop fooling around and get to the airport. You can buy the baby something special at Tiffany's—'

'Talie can take shorthand as fast I can, and she's fully briefed. I promise, you won't even miss me.'

Talie? Who the devil was Talie?

'Your daughter's got a partner, hasn't she? She doesn't need you to hold her hand—'

'Jude, I have to go.'

'I refuse to cope with some stranger. I want you. Here. Now!'

'She's not a stranger!' Then, 'Isn't she there? The car was supposed to have picked her up at nine-thirty.'

At that moment the automatic doors slid back, and as Jude Radcliffe caught sight of an unmistakable mop of blonde hair that even under restraint looked in danger of exploding he stopped listening. It was the pocket-sized blonde bombshell from the lift. She was pushing a trolley laden with a mountainous heap of luggage and talking to an elderly woman who was searching her handbag in a totally distracted manner.

'Heather,' he said, 'you're fired.'

And he cut the connection.

Talie, looking around desperately for someone in uniform to grab and ask for help, suddenly found herself confronted by her knight errant, freed from the armour of navy pinstripe and looking totally gorgeous in a grey cashmere sweater that exactly matched his eyes.

'Good heavens, are you going to New York, too? How brilliant! I thought I was going to be on my own with Jude Radcliffe, and everyone says he's a total…'

She stopped. The girls in the office might well be right, but it occurred to her that saying the first thing that came into her head might not be wise since, knight errant or not, he had to be one of Jude Radcliffe's famously bright young men. And, ignoring that enticing left eyebrow, which was inviting her to continue, she turned quickly to the elderly lady she'd rescued as she'd struggled with her trolley.

'This is Kitty,' she said. 'She's going to visit her new grandson in New Zealand. At least she would be if she could find her ticket.'

'It's all right, dear. I've found it. It was stuck between my book and my box of tissues.'

Talie breathed a huge sigh of relief as the woman finally produced the folder from the depths of her bag. 'I'll just take her to find her queue and then I'll be right back.'

'You're going nowhere. Our flight has already been called. You should have been here an hour ago.'

'I know, but there was an accident in the tunnel,' she said, a touch less brightly as it occurred to her that her knight might be dressed casually for travelling, but his expression was as unyielding as granite. Typical. Just when she could do with a smile or two to allay nerves that were stretched to breaking point, she finally got 'serious.'

'And you had to give first aid?' he enquired.

'Not this time,' she said, and, assuming he was teasing her, began to relax and smiled up at him. She was on her own with the smiling, she discovered. Losing her own rapidly, she said, 'I'll only be a minute—'

'You're not listening to me, Talie,' he said, in a tone that stopped her in her tracks.

'Oh, you know my name?'

'It's not a name. It's the word that goes in front of "ho."'

'It's short for Natalie,' she replied, refusing to allow him to rile her, furious with herself for being foolish enough to daydream for a whole week about riding in the lift again with him. 'The alternative is Nat,' she said. 'Which would you choose?'

There was a pause that lasted a heartbeat, no more.

'Talie what?'

'Calhoun,' she said, certain that she'd won a very small victory. But, refusing to fall into the trap of smiling again, she offered him her hand in her most businesslike manner. 'I'm standing in for Heather on this trip. Her daughter has—'

'I know what her daughter has done,' he said, taking her hand and clasping it in his, holding it a touch more firmly than was quite comfortable. Rather more 'You're not going anywhere' than 'How d'you do?' 'And I hope they run out of gas and air.'

'That's not very nice. I'm sure she didn't do it deliberately.' Then, seeing from his expression that she wasn't doing herself any favours, she said, 'I'm sorry, you have me at a disadvantage. You know my name, but I don't know yours.'

He didn't immediately fill the void, but instead gave her a look that took in her entire appearance, from the top of her embarrassing hair, via the comfortable trouser suit—it had been a toss-up between style and comfort and, taking into consideration the fact that she'd be sitting in it for seven hours, she'd gone for comfort—to her lowest heels. Right now she wished she'd gone for style, four-inch heels and to hell with practicality…

At that moment Kitty stopped fussing with her bag and looked up. 'Good Lord, aren't you Jude Radcliffe?' she said. 'I bought shares in your company after I saw you on TV. You were so charming when that nasty interviewer was rude to you…'

'Charm is all a matter of perspective. From Miss Calhoun's point of view I'm a total…' And that enticing left eyebrow invited her to fill in the blank.

The word that slipped from her lips wasn't the one she'd heard applied to him. But it was near enough.

CHAPTER TWO

'WELL,' Talie said, since she had to say something. 'Now we *both* know that I'm just as good at talking myself into trouble as out of it.'

It earned her a smile of sorts. The kind that said 'Now I've got you...' And she began to see how, while the 'sex-on-legs' tag fitted him to a *T*, he might not be the kind of man you'd want to work for.

Not that she anticipated having that particular problem for very long.

'Can you wait until I find out where Kitty needs to go before you sack me?' she asked.

'You're not getting off that lightly.' He snagged a passing female in a uniform with a glance—something she had signally failed to do with any number of glances—and said, 'Lady Milward is having trouble finding her check-in desk. Will you please take care of her?'

And then he really smiled. The full-scale, hundred-and-fifty-watt variety. The girl was putty by the time he'd reached sixty watts—if he'd looked at her like that Talie would have been putty—and she briefly considered a lecture on energy saving. Then decided she was in enough trouble...

'Have a good trip, Kitty,' he said, turning to the old lady and offering his hand. 'I hope to see you at the next shareholders' meeting.'

'You know her?' Talie demanded, having rescued her own luggage from Kitty's trolley before it was whisked away.

'When she said she was a shareholder I looked at her luggage

label. You were suckered, Talie Calhoun. But I don't suppose
you're the first person she's fooled with that helpless dithering
act. It's by getting other people to do their dirty work for them
for nothing that her kind got rich in the first place.'

'I don't care how much money she has,' Talie said, outraged.
'She needed help; I gave it.' And, since she had nothing to lose,
'What's made you so cynical?'

'Experience. Make a note to send her an invitation to the
cocktail party.'

A note? As in, like his personal assistant? And suddenly his
'You're not getting off that lightly,' made sense. Sacking her
would be too kind. She was going to have to work for him and
suffer.

In New York, she reminded herself. In New York.

'Which cocktail party?' she asked.

'The one we hold for shareholders after the Annual General
Meeting.'

'Right.' She made a move to dig out her notebook.

'A mental note. We have to check in before they close the
flight.'

He picked up the cheap-and-cheerful holdall that had seen her
through her student days but which looked embarrassingly
scruffy next to the wheel-on laptop bag that Heather had sent
with the car, and placed it beside his own equally worn leather
holdall.

The thing about buying quality, she thought, was that it
matured with age. The scuffs lent it character. Unlike cheap-and-
cheerful which, once past its cheerful stage, just looked—well,
cheap.

'Passport.' He held out his hand for it as they reached the first-
class check-in desk.

He had good hands. Large enough to be comforting, with long
fingers and the kind of broad-tipped thumb that... Well, never
mind what the thumb suggested to her overheated imagination.

But you could tell a lot from a man by looking at his hands.
His lied.

She handed over her passport and tickets. The clerk already
had all the details of the change of passenger in her computer, so

there was no delay, and it occurred to her that, for a woman distracted by the difficulties of her daughter's labour, Heather had done an amazing job of handling the details so that Jude Radcliffe's life would proceed as smoothly as if she was there herself.

It was scarcely surprising that he was irritated to discover that instead of perfection he'd been lumbered with her. Maybe she was being a little harsh. Stifling a yawn, she made a silent vow not to do anything to annoy him further as she and the wheel-on laptop bag put in the occasional hop and skip in an attempt to keep pace with him as he strode towards the boarding gate, making no concession to the fact that her legs were at least a foot shorter than his.

She revised her earlier regret about her shoes, too.

In four-inch heels she'd never have made it.

She also vowed to keep her mouth shut. Not speak unless she was spoken to.

It wasn't easy. Her student travelling had been done using the cross-Channel ferry and backpacking across Europe, which she'd loved. Her one and only experience of flying was cattle-class on a package tour charter flight, and she'd hated every minute of it.

But this was different, and despite her apprehension—she refused to admit to the flutter of anxiety that until now she'd been too distracted to notice—she looked about her, eager to enthuse about the size of the seats, the amount of space each passenger had and the neat little individual television screens. She always talked too much when she was nervous.

Biting her lower lip to keep her mouth shut, she explored her space, picking up the entertainment programme. 'We get a choice of films?' she asked, forgetting her vow of silence in her astonishment.

'Other people might. You are here to work.'

For seven solid hours?

'Of course. I was merely making an observation,' she said crisply, and, restricting her enthusiasm to the business at hand, she opened the laptop bag. 'This is the note that Heather sent you, Mr Radcliffe,' she said, handing him an envelope. 'To explain about me.'

'I know all about you,' he said, without enthusiasm. 'You watch romantic films, attract trouble and are always late.'

This was definitely a moment for silence.

Satisfied, he said, 'And you will call me Jude.'

'Oh, but I couldn't!'

Well, that didn't last long...

'Try,' Jude insisted, trying very hard to keep his temper. Why on earth had Heather picked this woman as her stand-in? It was bad enough that he'd found himself constantly distracted by the memory of those few seconds they'd spent together in the lift, wasting time he'd allocated to thinking about the direction in which he should take the company during the next five years.

Instead of planning corporate strategy he'd been thinking about her ridiculous hair. That totally infectious smile...

He needed someone he could trust on this trip, and Heather was the one who'd suggested that this girl might have been putting on an act, for heaven's sake. That her story had been just that. A story to snag his attention.

Except he'd just seen her in action. If she was that good an actress she was wasting her time in an office. But somehow the fact that her compassion, her enthusiasm for life, wasn't an act disturbed him far more. He was more comfortable with guile. Understood it. Knew how to handle it.

He took a slow breath. He was stuck with her and they'd both have to live with it.

'I may be a bastard,' he said. 'Although my mother might take issue with you on that. And I certainly don't suffer fools in any shape or form in my organisation. But Heather calls me Jude and so will you.' Then, in case she was under any misapprehension that he was being friendly—he was deeply regretting his uncharacteristic impulse to hold the lift for her— 'That way I won't be constantly reminded of her absence every time you speak.'

And, without waiting for her to reply, he opened the envelope and took out a single folded sheet of paper. The note was brief and to the point.

Jude, I know you're going to be furious that I've had to miss this trip, but you know you're going to have to get used to working without me in the near future. I gave you a year to find a replacement and time is running out. And, no, I didn't do this deliberately. Even you must realise that I can't control the arrival of an impatient baby.

Just don't take it out on Talie. It's not her fault. Mike raved about her. She takes shorthand verbatim, and I took the trouble to check out her story about the incident on the Underground last week. Unlikely as it may seem, your little blonde was telling the truth.

I know—she's almost too good to be true. But I'm sure a week working for you will bring out any hidden flaws. If you behave yourself, you might even be able to persuade her to take you on full time. Heather.

He glanced down at the girl sitting beside him. 'Heather suggests you're almost too good to be true. Shall we see if she's right?'

'What?'

It was just as well her eyes were blue or he'd be forced to compare them with a startled doe's.

What an appallingly banal thought.

At least she'd made an effort to get her hair under control, stuffing it up into some kind of knot on the top of her head that was not so much a bun, more a cottage loaf. Even as he congratulated himself a curl sprang free, refusing to be confined by anything so feeble as a hairpin.

Realising that she was still staring up at him like a startled blue-eyed—and there really was no other word for it—doe, he said, 'If you'd like to get out your notebook some time before we arrive in New York, maybe I can find out if you're as good as Mike and Heather claim you are,' he prompted.

'But we haven't even taken off…' She caught her bottom lip between her teeth, presumably to prevent the rest of the sentence from escaping and thus provoking further sarcasm.

And that irritated him, too. He felt like being seriously—

'Would you fasten your seat-belts, please?' a stewardess said as she walked through the cabin, checking that everything was properly stowed. 'We'll be taking off shortly.'

Talie, it seemed, had a firm grasp of the priorities and got out her notebook before she fastened her seat-belt, made a note of the time and date, wrote something else in shorthand—probably what she wanted to say out loud but thought it wiser not to—and then turned to him, her pencil poised and waiting.

'Whenever you're ready,' she said. 'Jude.'

He dragged his attention from her hair, which was slowly unravelling, and began to dictate a series of notes on the ideas he'd had during his solitary days walking in the Scottish Highlands. The ones that didn't involve the dimple that appeared for no reason at all every now and then at the corner of her mouth.

The plane backed slowly away from the gate before taxiing to the runway. There was a long pause as they waited for clearance and, glancing across to ensure that she was keeping up with him, he noticed that the knuckles of the hand gripping her pencil were bone-white.

She was nervous? This girl who, without a second thought, leapt to the aid of total strangers in distress?

As he hesitated, she glanced up at him. It wasn't only her knuckles that were white, he realised, and as the engine noise grew and the plane began to speed down the runway he stepped up the speed at which he was dictating in an effort to distract her.

It might have worked, too, but when a day started out badly, it invariably kept going that way, and as they lifted off something crashed loose in the galley behind them. A woman in the aisle seat opposite them gave a startled scream and Talie jumped so violently that she would undoubtedly have left her seat if she hadn't been strapped in. As it was, her notebook and pencil took off on a flight of their own, and the pins which had been struggling manfully with gravity to hold up her hair gave up the effort and the cottage loaf exploded.

'Are we going to die?' she whispered.

'Yes,' he said, reaching out and taking her hand. 'But not today.'

He really was a bastard, Talie decided, as her heart rate slowly returned to normal. How could she ever have imagined for one minute that he was friendly? Charming? Totally scrummy, actually.

She had practically haunted the lifts of the Radcliffe Tower in her lunchtimes, hoping to run into him again. Knowing that she was being stupid. Just how stupid she couldn't possibly have imagined.

Okay. She'd give him the killer good looks—even if he was using those slate eyes to freeze her to her seat—and she was right about his hands. They were strong and capable and very good for holding on to when you thought your last moment had come.

Admittedly he'd lost the smooth, boyish look of the average pop idol, and settled into that look men achieved around their mid to late thirties and hung on to until the muscles started to sag a little around the jaw, when they were so old that it didn't matter. When he smiled he didn't look anywhere near old enough to be the ill-tempered tycoon described by her colleagues.

Unable to rescue her notebook until the seat-belt sign went off, Talie remained absolutely still, trying to ignore the warmth of his palm pressed against hers, the way his long fingers curled reassuringly around her hand. Instead she closed her eyes and re-ran their encounter in the lift, trying to work out how she could have got it so wrong.

He'd seemed friendly enough, but then she hadn't given him much of a chance to be anything else, prattling on about being late. He probably wouldn't have spoken to her at all under normal circumstances. Most of his staff probably wouldn't have dared say anything beyond good morning.

None of them would have yelled at him to hold the lift. They'd rather have been late.

And he wasn't being funny when he said she could talk her way out of anything, she realised belatedly. He was being sarcastic.

The seat-belt sign pinged off, but before she could move, reclaim her notepad, he had released her hand and picked it up for her.

'Have you stopped shaking sufficiently to carry on?' he asked, handing it to her. 'Or do you require a medicinal brandy?'

'If I had a medicinal brandy that would be the end of my working day,' she said. 'Not the beginning of it.'

She looked around for her pencil, but it had rolled away under a seat somewhere, and since she wasn't about to crawl around on her hands and knees looking for it she took a new one from her bag. Then, suspecting that she might need more than one, she swiftly anchored her hair back into place and stuck some spares into the resulting bird's nest, so that she wouldn't have to cut him off in full flow.

'Whenever you're ready,' she said. Then, when he didn't immediately begin, she glanced up at him and realised that he was staring at her hair. For just a moment she thought he was going to make some seriously cutting remark.

Maybe she was mistaken. Or maybe he'd wisely thought better of it. Because after a moment he sat back, closed his eyes and continued pouring his thoughts out at a rate that kept her fully occupied for some time.

Her attention briefly wandered when an infant whose mother was deeply engrossed in the film she was watching caught her eye and with a giggle tossed a drinking cup in her direction, hoping for a playmate.

Any other time she'd have been there…

The cup rolled away down the aisle and the child started to cry. Talie found it really, really hard to stay put when every instinct was urging her to leap up and retrieve it. Instead she took a deep breath and, as she turned the page, hit the buzzer to attract the attention of the stewardess.

'Good decision,' Jude said.

She'd written it down before she realised that it was a comment rather than dictation. Clearly his eyes weren't as firmly closed as she'd imagined.

The flight passed without further incident. She typed up the notes Jude had dictated until the laptop battery beeped a warning that it was about to go flat. But if she thought all she had to do was hit 'save' and then relax for the rest of the flight, she was mistaken.

Jude stopped working on some figures, took a special adapter from his own laptop bag and leaned across her to plug it into the power outlet of the aircraft—obviously concerned that she'd do fatal damage to the aircraft electronics if he left her to do it herself.

He might be an unmitigated bastard as a boss, but he did have gorgeous hair, she thought with an envious sigh as she got an unexpected close-up. Dark as bitter chocolate, perfectly cut so that every silky strand knew its place. Even the lick that momentarily slid across his forehead needed no encouragement to return to order.

She tucked a stray curl behind her ear and comforted herself with the thought that good hair wasn't everything.

Kindness was much more important.

He refused all offers of tea, coffee, even lunch when it arrived, and, taking only water, kept working. She had no idea if he expected her to follow his example, but enough was enough. He might be able to function on fresh air, but she needed a substantial amount of calories if she was going to keep up this level of output. She made a mental note to stock up on an emergency supply of chocolate at the first confectionery outlet she passed.

After the stewardess had removed her tray, he began again. This time dictating notes for an after-dinner speech he was going to make to some business group, stopping just before her right hand began to scream for mercy.

She began to wonder if Heather's daughter had really gone into early labour. She might just have decided that she could do with a break, and could always say it had been a false alarm…

Mentally slapping herself for having such evil thoughts, she applied herself to the keyboard, and was taken by surprise when the Captain announced that they would shortly be arriving at JFK.

'I don't believe it! A yellow cab!'

Jude glanced across the road to where a constant stream of cabs was picking up new arrivals. 'No, you're right. It's yellow.' Then, spotting his driver climbing out of a waiting limo, he said, 'This is our car.'

He ignored her disappointment that they weren't going to drive into Manhattan in one of New York's landmark institutions. It wasn't his business to fulfil her tourist fantasies.

'Barney, Heather couldn't come this trip. Talie is standing in for her, so you'll need to liaise with her about when you'll be needed.'

'Pleased to know you, Talie,' Barney said, with a wide smile. 'First time in New York?'

'Yes,' she said, beaming back. 'I can't wait to see the city.'

'Well, you climb in and buckle up now, while I take care of those bags, and we'll have you there in no time.'

She kept her notebook and the briefing file with her, and since, apart from the yellow cabs, the airport surroundings offered nothing more to interest her, she glanced through the crowded schedule for the trip. 'You have a meeting with your U.S. team at four o'clock.' Then, with a frown, 'That is so weird. We've already had four o'clock once today. I guess that's jet lag.'

'You would only have had four o'clock once if you'd changed your watch to New York time as soon as we took off.'

'Er—when?' she asked.

He didn't bother pretending to misunderstand her. 'You found time for lunch,' he pointed out. And she'd found time to re-pin her hair, too. His concentration had been ruined by the constant threat of a second detonation of hairpins. But their landing had been incident free and her curls had remained firmly anchored. He dragged his gaze from them with some difficulty. 'And you've no need to worry about jet lag. I promise you won't have any time to suffer from that.'

'Well, that's a relief. I was worried there…' Her mouth twitched, as if she was trying very hard to control a smile. 'Just for a minute.'

Humour? Well, fine. They'd see how long she could keep that up.

'And I don't have a meeting at four o'clock,' he pointed out. '*We* have a meeting a four o'clock.'

'You want me to take notes?' If she'd thought about it she would have assumed the New York office would supply someone to do that. In fact she didn't understand why the New York office couldn't supply him with all the secretarial support he needed.

'I'm not taking you along as a fashion accessory. Somehow I don't see pencils in the hair catching on in—'

But he could see that he'd lost her, and he turned to see what she was looking at.

It was, of course, the Manhattan skyline, hazy and golden in the early-afternoon sunshine. Right ahead of them the Empire State Building towered over the city, and a little away to the left the sun was striking off the polished art deco roof of the Chrysler Building.

It was the hackneyed subject of a thousand picture postcards, and he'd seen it so many times that it had lost any power to hold him, but Talie Calhoun was clearly entranced. She gave a little sigh of pure pleasure and said, 'I can't believe I'm actually looking at the Empire State Building. Going to the top is number one on my list of things to do while I'm here.'

'If you want to be a tourist, Talie,' he said, irritated that he'd lost her attention to a cliché, 'you're going to have to book a package holiday and do it on your own time. While you're here with me I'll want you available twenty-four/seven.'

Those blue eyes flashed back at him, and for a moment he thought she was going to give him an argument. Remind him that all he could demand of her was an eight-hour day—and he'd already had that and more.

Common sense won, although a mutinous lower lip trembled with outrage, fighting a fierce rearguard battle as she tried to clamp it tight against its more restrained upper partner.

He was almost sorry. He would have given a lot to know exactly what she was thinking right at that moment.

But then he'd have had to fire her, too.

CHAPTER THREE

TALIE clenched her jaw to keep her mouth from saying what was in her mind. She was professional. She could be cool. She knew that working on an overseas trip was not a nine-to-five deal. But she also knew that there was no way he was going to keep her occupied for every minute, day and night.

Even Jude Radcliffe had to sleep.

She would get to the top of the Empire State Building even if it was the only item she achieved on her wish list. She'd get someone to take a photograph of her while she was there, too. Then she'd send him a copy when they were safely home in London and leave him to wonder how she'd found the time.

But in the meantime she would be good. And since he had finally stopped issuing orders and pouring out dictation—it was likely that even *his* brain needed some down time in order to fill up with more words—she sat very still and enjoyed the rest of the ride into Upper Manhattan. She was thrilled by it all, even the worn-out buildings that skirted all big cities, and was finally rewarded with tantalising glimpses of narrow streets with pretty sidewalks that could have come straight from any Woody Allen movie.

She just about managed to bottle up her astonishment that the roads were so narrow. Or was it just the height of the buildings that made them appear that way? And she barely let out a squeak as she caught her first sight of Central Park, with the horse-drawn buggies lined up to give romantic rides through the park. It was so frustrating not to be able to share her enthusiasm with Jude.

'Was that on your list, too?'

Obviously it had been enough of a squeak to alert him to further 'tourist' ambitions.

'Sorry?' She tried to appear absolutely cool, as if she had no idea what Jude was talking about. It clearly wasn't working, so before that wretched eyebrow could go into overdrive she said, 'Oh, you mean a buggy ride in the park? No. It wouldn't be much fun doing it on my own.'

'No,' he said, after a moment. 'I don't suppose it would.' Then, as the car slowed to a halt in front of their hotel. 'Okay, you've got twenty minutes to freshen up before we leave.'

'Do you want me to deal with the check-in formalities?' she asked, as the bellman took their bags and summoned a lift.

'It isn't necessary. I keep a permanent suite here. It's less bother than an apartment.'

'Of course it is,' she said. And didn't even try to keep the irony from her voice. His payback came when he used a swipe key to open the door, then stood back to let her go ahead of him.

Her mouth didn't actually drop open, but only because she was already so deep in jaw-drop mode at finding herself in such surroundings that she had it tightly clamped shut for safety.

His suite had all the extravagant trappings she had ever seen in the movies she watched day after day with her mother. The luxurious furniture, a carpet that seemed to swallow her feet, flowers and fruit...

It even had its own little kitchen. And, less enticingly, the latest office technology set up in a mini-office.

But the stunning view of Central Park from her bedroom window cancelled out this reminder that she was here to work. Not that she had much time to linger over the view.

It didn't matter. Nothing and no one—not even Jude Radcliffe—could wipe the huge grin that was riveted to her face as she dived into the shower.

She was in New York!

'Have you ever considered doing something with your hair?' Jude enquired as they drove downtown. Her quick shower had reduced it to a mass of corkscrew curls that not even the toughest pin could hold down.

'What kind of something?' she enquired, looking up at him with an innocent look that he didn't believe in for a moment. He was beginning to get the measure of Talie Calhoun.

'Something involving the use of sharp scissors?' he offered.

'It has been tried,' she said, not unkindly, but as if explaining something to a fool. 'My hair, as you can imagine, was a trial to my mother, and once—after breaking yet another comb—she hacked it short with her dressmaking shears. It gave a whole new meaning to the description "poodle cut."'

He suspected he was supposed to laugh. Instead he found himself confronted by the pitiable image of a very small Talie, with her hair chopped off in uneven chunks, and wished he had kept his mouth shut.

'I had something a little more professional in mind,' he said, rather more gently.

'An expensive poodle cut?' she responded, not letting him off that easily.

'Okay,' he said, deciding to get the apology over and done with. 'Point taken. I shouldn't have—'

'I did briefly consider going for broke with a Number One,' she continued, as if he hadn't spoken. 'But the problem then would be that I'd be stuck with it forever, because I would never willingly go through the nightmare stage of growing it out.' Then, 'Of course, if you have any other suggestions I'd be happy to hear them. In the meantime, look on the bright side. If I wear it loose I can't park my pencils in it.'

For once in his life he couldn't think of a thing to say. His mistake had been to break every rule in his own handbook for dealing with people and get involved. He didn't even bother to try again with the apology. She'd matched him and then some, and he spent the rest of the journey with his mouth firmly closed while his mind—which had far more important things to concern it—wasted precious time wondering what on earth she was doing temping when she was not only hard-working, but smart enough to put him in his place without raising a sweat.

She seemed to have the same effect on everyone else when she walked into the boardroom and half a dozen of the least impressionable men he knew temporarily lost the power of speech.

'Gentlemen, this is Talie Calhoun. Heather is busy becoming a grandmother, and Talie is standing in for her on this trip.' About to say that they should give her every assistance, he realised it was unnecessary. He was more likely to be trampled in the crush as his staff overcame their initial shocked surprise and vied to shake her hand, offer her coffee, carry her bag.

He firmly resisted the foolish urge to beat them off, instead leaving them to introduce themselves while his lawyer updated him on the latest situation with the company they were planning to take over.

Talie had expected Jude to call the meeting to order, but since he was otherwise occupied she just smiled and enjoyed being the centre of attention while it lasted.

'Did you have a good flight, Talie?' a tall, tanned god-like figure asked, after he'd introduced himself.

'I didn't notice,' she said. 'I was working.'

'Any flight you don't notice is good flight,' another man said. Tall—they were all so damned tall she'd get a crick in her neck from looking up—dark and with the inbred confidence of a male who only had to smile to get what he wanted. 'Hi, I'm Marcus Wade.'

'How d'you do, Mr Wade?' she replied politely, taking the hand he offered.

'Marcus,' he said, not shaking her hand, just holding it.

'Oh, wow. I love that accent. Say something else,' said a voice behind her.

She turned her head—short of wrenching her hand from Marcus she had no other option—and smiled at a third, younger man. 'How now brown cow?' she offered, her consonants crisp, her diphthongs BBC-perfect. He pretended to swoon and she laughed.

'Is this your first visit to New York?' This from a drool-worthy Brad Pitt look-alike. Make that all so tall *and* good-looking, she thought. They all looked so...wholesome. Except Marcus Wade. He had that bad-boy look that gave the mothers of impressionable girls the shivers. Fortunately, she was no longer a girl, and she'd never been that easily impressed. At least not until a recent ride in a lift. And that had proved how dangerous first impressions could be...

'Yes. It's amazing. I still can't believe I'm here.'

'Well, that's wonderful. You've got it all to see for the first time. The Statue of Liberty, Central Park, Times Square—'

'The first thing you have to do is take a boat trip around the harbour,' someone else pitched in.

'And a bus tour—'

'Actually, I don't think I'm going to have time—'

'Sunday brunch at Katz's is a must. You are going to be here over the weekend, aren't you? I'd be happy to take you.' This from Marcus, reclaiming her attention. And now he wasn't smiling; he was totally serious. As if this was the most important thing in the entire world at that moment. She was good and didn't laugh. Instead she said, 'That's really very sweet of you, but—'

'Sweet! She said "sweet"…priceless!'

Marcus didn't seem to think it was priceless. He just glowered at the man who thought it was…

'But we're leaving on Thursday morning,' she finished.

'But you'll have time to see a show?' the B.P. look-alike, sensing an opportunity, immediately leapt in. 'You *have* to see a show—'

Jude found himself distracted by the knot of eager young men clustered around Talie and glanced across, intending to call the meeting to order. Instead he caught a glimpse of her and forgot what he was about to say.

She'd abandoned the shapeless trouser suit and flat shoes for a charcoal-grey suit that skimmed her old-fashioned hourglass figure, high heels that drew attention to a pair of the classiest ankles he'd ever seen, and her hair was lit up like a halo by a bright ray of sun striking in through the window.

'—and the Empire State after dark. That's a must. We'll do it tonight, Talie. Dinner first, after the meeting, and then I'll take you for a ride to the top of the world—'

'Not this evening, Marcus,' he said abruptly. 'Talie has a prior engagement with a computer, and I'm sure you'll have plenty to occupy you, too.'

'You don't let her eat?'

Jude found himself being challenged by one of his brightest

young men—not, as he'd anticipated, for power, but for the attention of a girl. He would soon learn to choose his battles with more care. Save his big moves for something that mattered.

There was always another girl.

'It was Jude who worked through lunch today, not me,' Talie said, glancing at her hand so pointedly that Marcus could do nothing but surrender it. 'Can I get anyone coffee before we start? Jude?'

Burying his annoyance that she'd leapt, quite unnecessarily, to his defence, he said, 'No. Let's get on.' He indicated that she should sit beside him, and then tried to forget about her as they began to thrash out the details of strategy for the following week.

It wasn't easy.

It was impossible to be unaware of the fact that whenever he spoke he had a rapt audience. Maybe it was unswerving interest in the business at hand, but he had the uncomfortable feeling that it was Talie's presence beside him that fixed their attention. He'd never had to compete with a bunch of testosterone-driven young executives for Heather's attention. Or with her for theirs, he thought, as he glanced down at Talie to ensure that she wasn't flagging and caught her exchanging a smile with someone.

But then Heather was about to become a grandmother, he reminded himself as they finally broke for sandwiches and coffee. Talie was swamped with offers of help as she poured and served, although he noticed that Marcus was doing a pretty good job of keeping all comers at bay, blocking their moves with his footballer's shoulders as he whispered something in her ear.

He'd been Jude's first choice to run the New York office. Unstoppable when he wanted something, his charm disguising the essential ruthless edge.

Talie threw back her head as she laughed at something he'd said, at which point Jude stopped congratulating himself and abruptly called the meeting back to order.

'What are you doing about dinner, Jude?' Marcus said, as the meeting finally broke up. 'I can call that Italian restaurant you like and see if they can give us a table.'

'If you think your day is done, Marcus, by all means go out and enjoy yourself,' he said, not fooled for a minute by this apparently casual invitation. There was only one person Marcus wanted to have dinner with, and if he couldn't extract her from Jude's side then he was confident enough of his power to charm to invite the whole group along. 'We are less fortunate. Talie has notes to type up, and I have plenty to keep me busy, so we'll have to make do with Room Service tonight.'

'That was terribly cruel,' she said, as they made their way out of the building.

'Cruel?'

'What you did to Marcus. He'll carry on working all night, now.'

'I've no doubt that's what he'll tell me he did,' he said. 'But I'm prepared to bet that it won't be more than half an hour before he's on his way to some classy little restaurant.' He resisted the temptation to add that he wouldn't be alone. It would make too much of nothing. It would suggest it mattered.

'Lucky him,' Talie said.

'You're hungry?'

She glanced up at him, and for a moment he thought she was going to say something important. She clearly had second thoughts, because she just shook her head. 'To be honest, I think I've gone past food. I'd rather just get on with typing up the minutes and then go to bed. I am allowed to sleep?'

'If you don't want to eat, I suggest you do just that.'

She didn't say a word, but her look spoke volumes.

'You'll be wide awake at three o'clock,' he said. 'You can catch up then.'

'You're all heart,' she said, climbing into the back of the limo.

'Hearts are for losers, Talie. There are no dividends for being soft. The only thing you can rely on in this world is money,' he said. 'The deal.'

'Nobody can be that cynical,' she said.

He didn't bother to argue, and when, a few minutes after she'd retired, apparently too tired to keep her eyes open, he heard the phone ring in her room just once before it was snatched up, he decided that cynicism served him very well.

CHAPTER FOUR

'TALIE, will you call Room Service—?'

Jude's heart had lifted in anticipation of her bright presence, hard at work transcribing the notes of the meeting while the printer busily churned out all the stuff she'd typed up on the plane. But the printer was quiet, the laptop closed and, far from sitting at the desk working, his secretary was notable only by her absence.

'Talie?'

It was after seven a.m. He'd relied on the time difference to have him awake long before now—but then he hadn't gone to bed until the early hours. Talie didn't have that excuse, and when there was no answer from her room he rapped sharply on her door to rouse her, then took a bottle of water from the fridge. When, after he'd taken a long draught, there was still no sound of movement from her bedroom, he knocked again before opening the door.

There was no sound because she wasn't there, which was disturbing enough. But what rocked him back was the fact that her bed looked as if it hadn't been slept in.

He didn't know what made him angrier. That Marcus had been wasting time lusting after her when he should have been concentrating on the job in hand. Or that Talie had been stupid enough to fall for his smooth act.

Her only desire might have been to see the world from the top of New York's best-known building, but anyone could have seen that he had something much more intimate in mind.

The phone in his own bedroom interrupted his black fury and he snatched it up. 'Yes!'

'This is Vince from Security, Mr Radcliffe. We have...a situation.'

Talie. It could only be Talie... 'What kind of a situation?'

'Well, sir, we're holding a young lady here who's asked for a key to your suite. She says she's your PA, and while obviously she's lying—we all know Mrs Lester—I thought perhaps I should check with you. Before I take it any further.'

The delicacy with which this was put left him in no doubt what the man was thinking, and he was sorely tempted to leave Talie Calhoun to cool her heels for a while in Security. If nothing else, it would make him feel better. And teach her not to try and creep back in undetected after a night on the tiles.

Unfortunately he didn't have the time for that, but she could sweat it out for a few more minutes.

'I'll come down, Vince.'

And, replacing the receiver, he pulled on his sweats. While Little Miss Tourist was typing herself back into his good books he'd put in some time at the hotel gym.

'This is totally outrageous!'

He heard her before he opened the door.

'Please, ma'am, stay calm...'

'Calm! Have you any idea how I felt, being escorted from Reception into the security office with everyone looking at me as if I was some kind of crook, or a hotel thief, or a...a...a professional lady?' Her voice exploded on the final category.

'Now, ma'am, there's no need to get angry. We'll get this sorted—'

'You think this is angry?' she demanded.

She was standing in the middle of the security office, confronting three of the hotel's security officers, all of whom towered over her, and she wasn't giving an inch.

'This isn't angry. This is mildly irritated—'

'Talie? What's the problem?'

She turned at the sound of his voice. 'Jude. Thank goodness. What the devil took you so long?' For a moment the fierceness in her voice wobbled, betraying her fear, and he wanted to just reach out and hold her. Tell her it was okay... But before he could move she rallied. 'Why didn't you just tell him that it was okay? When he phoned?' She indicated the older of the men.

'I was coming down anyway, so I thought it would be better to reassure Vince in person.'

As he had anticipated, she had discarded the business suit, but she wasn't wearing some sexy little number with which to ensnare his young protégé. Instead she was dressed in a thin grey T-shirt that clung enticingly to her curves and a pair of cut-off jogging pants that displayed a disturbing amount of smooth, tanned leg.

And her hair—it was always the hair that dominated her appearance—was tumbling out of the band she'd used to tie it back and sticking damply to her face.

'Forget Vince! All you had to say was, "If she's short, mouthy and has bad hair she's okay,"' she said, hands on hips as she turned and he became the target of her fury.

He was finding it difficult to stop himself from laughing, but knew she'd never forgive him if he did that, so he said, 'Vince, may I introduce Miss Talie Calhoun, who's standing in for Mrs Lester this week?' And then he did smile. 'She's okay. Could you sort out a swipe card for her, please?'

'Yes, sir.'

And suddenly no one seemed to find it necessary to hang around. Once they were on their own, he turned back to Talie.

'A *professional* lady?' he prompted.

Her cheeks, already pink, flushed a darker shade. Clearly the same impetuosity that had her leaping to the rescue of the halt and confused drove her tongue.

'I really don't think you need have worried on that score,' he said.

She instantly rallied. 'I was over-ambitious, you think?'

A strand of hair was corkscrewing wildly over her left eye. She blew it away but it fell back and, quite unable to stop himself, he reached out and tucked it behind her ear, holding it there.

'I think I'll pass on that one.' Then, realising that he was at risk of crossing a very dangerous line, he took a step back and, moving swiftly on, said, 'Where the devil have you been?'

She regarded him as if he was insane, before looking down at her clothes in a gesture that suggested he figure it out for himself. Then, presumably in case he was terminally thick, she said, 'I've been for a run.'

All night?

'On your own?' he asked, suddenly a lot more concerned for her safety than her morals.

'Is there some law against it?' Then, 'Look, I finally gave up trying to sleep at about four, typed up your notes and printed them out, and then I just wanted some fresh air—okay?'

'You've done *everything?*'

'You did say—'

'I know what I said. I didn't actually mean it.'

'Didn't you? Oh.'

She lifted her shoulders in something that wasn't quite a shrug but conveyed the same message. Why would she have doubted that he'd meant exactly what he said?

'I'm sorry. I'm so used to working with Heather—'

'No, it's okay. You were right. I was wide awake, and it was pointless just lying there waiting for the sun to come up.'

'So you typed up the minutes and then went for a run in Central Park?'

'In company with dozens of other people, so you needn't worry about me behaving like a "tourist,"' she said, making quote marks with her fingers. 'I was behaving like a gen-yoo-ine New Yorker.' Then, eyeing his sweats, 'If you'd woken up in time you could have come with me. Did you take a sleeping pill or something? I knocked as loudly as I could—'

'Why didn't you take the swipe card? It was on the desk.'

'I did, but I put it in my bum bag with my camera and I think the battery might have corrupted the magnetic strip. When I couldn't rouse you, I came back down here for a new one. Which is when I was "invited" to step into the security office.'

The manager himself returned, with two fresh swipe card keys. 'My apologies for the confusion, Mr Radcliffe,' he said. 'Mrs Lester telephoned to let us know you'd both be arriving yesterday. No one informed us that there had been a change of plan—'

'Amazing. I thought the woman was infallible,' Talie muttered.

'…and naturally the reception clerk chose caution.'

'Of course, Mr Luis. It is entirely our fault—'

'Don't do that! Don't apologise to him. I'm the one who was treated like something untouchable,' Talie said, clearly believing—with some justification—that any apology should be offered to her. 'I have no doubt everyone would have been a lot politer if I'd been wearing designer running shoes that cost more money than I get paid for an entire week's work,' she said. Then, sweetly, 'Of course if I'd been a real crook I could have afforded them.'

'I'm sure everyone will treat you with the utmost respect in future,' Jude said, placing his hand firmly on her back and easing her through the door. Then, when there was a safe distance between it and them, 'You do realise that you have given me more trouble in two days than Heather has given me in ten years?'

She looked surprised—with good reason, since most of the disturbance was in his mind—and opened her mouth as if about to challenge him, before obviously thinking better of it. Instead she took a deep breath and said, 'This time the trouble really wasn't my fault.'

'I know, but the guy was just doing his job,' he said unsympathetically. 'Get over it.'

'Right,' she said, and, after another deep breath, 'Absolutely. I'll go back and apologise when I'm cleaned up.' Then, as they reached the lifts, 'I really am sorry I embarrassed you, but I was scared I was going to be thrown into a police cell.'

'I'd have bailed you out,' he promised. 'Eventually.'

She grinned. 'Yes, okay. I'm catching on. You're not as bad as everyone says…' Then, swiftly changing the subject, 'Honestly—look at me.' Her snit over as quickly as it had blown up, a smile tugged at the corner of her mouth, that elusive dimple tempting him to see things from her point of view. 'What did the wretched man think I was going to do to you?'

He looked. And felt an overwhelming urge to grin right back.

'I can't imagine,' he lied, overwhelmed with images of any manner of things she might do to him.

And he rapidly lost any desire to laugh.

'Here's your key,' he said, as he summoned a lift for her.

'Don't keep this one with your camera.' Despite himself, he was unable to resist calling her on her insistence that she was behaving like a local. 'Do you usually take it with you when you go for a run?'

'Absolutely,' she replied, all wide-eyed innocence. 'Doesn't everyone?' Then, with a grin, 'All right, it's a fair cop. I was being a total tourist, but I wanted some snaps of yellow cabs and skyscrapers, and that bridge where the old lady lived in the movie *Home Alone*—the Christmas one. And the place where everyone goes ice skating in the winter.'

'And which movie did you see that in?'

'*Serendipity*...' Then, 'Oh, you are sooo smart, Jude Radcliffe,' she said, laughing. 'They're not for me. I wanted them for my mother.'

'Of course you did.'

'No, honestly...' And while the smile was still fixed in place, and would have fooled the casual observer into believing she was the happiest girl alive, her eyes were no longer joining in. 'She's the movie fan. I didn't know if I'd get another chance to take pictures.'

'You're a bright woman. I have no doubt you'll find a way to get exactly what you want. I'll be in the gym for the next thirty minutes or so, if anyone is desperate to get hold of me,' he said as the lift arrived, glad of an excuse to walk away. He didn't want to know what had evoked those shadows. All he was interested in was that she did her job.

'A run outside in the fresh air would do you more good,' she called after him, holding the lift door.

'But this way I can watch CNN and get the latest stock prices at the same time.'

'That's got to be a recipe for a heart attack. Do you want me to order breakfast for you?'

On the point of asking her to have some freshly squeezed orange juice sent up, he found himself saying, 'We're in New York, Talie. Don't you know that gen-yoo-ine New Yorkers go out for breakfast?'

'Do they? How bizarre.'

'This from the woman who snaps as she jogs?'

'I'm a sad female with an incurable tourist habit, Jude. Get over it,' she said, claiming the last word for herself as the lift doors closed.

But at least the sparkle was back in her eyes.

CHAPTER FIVE

'So, what do you do apart from watch films, Talie?'

They'd walked to a small café where she had proceeded to wipe out all the good she'd done with her early-morning exercise by completely letting herself go and ordering crisp bacon, scrambled eggs and pancakes with maple syrup. And a side order of blueberries.

'Blueberries are really good for your eyesight,' she'd assured Jude. Not that he'd said anything. But that eyebrow...

'In that case better make that everything for two,' he'd told the waitress who'd brought their coffee and orange juice. Then, when she didn't leap in to fill the silence as she usually did, he'd asked her what she did besides watch films.

'Run,' she offered, suddenly wishing she'd just acted on her own initiative and ordered Room Service for both of them. Back in the suite he would have been concentrating on work. And so would she. They could have sniped at one another happily enough, without time to be distracted by personal details. But the buzz that had surged through her when he'd suggested going out to breakfast had nothing to do with the opportunity to behave like a New Yorker. She'd wanted him to notice her...

Dangerous.

No. Worse than dangerous. Stupid.

'Okay, you run...what else do you do?' he persisted.

She stopped toying with her spoon.

'I like to cook,' she said—that was safe. She looked up, faced him. 'And I do a little needlework.'

'Needlework?'

He didn't sound convinced. Maybe that had been pushing the bounds of credibility a little too far.

'I once started a sampler,' she assured him. 'It was for my Brownie needlework badge...'

He was supposed to laugh. He didn't. Instead he continued to regard her intently, as if he'd suddenly realised that she was a person, with thoughts and feelings. She'd felt a lot safer when he was being an irritable bastard. She could ignore that...

'Well, that's covered your hobbies. What about your life?'

'Oh, I *see*.' He wanted to know about her life. That was more difficult, because she didn't actually have a *life*—not the way he meant it, anyway. 'You want to know who I sleep with.'

He regarded her for a moment, but she had absolutely no idea what he was thinking, which was disconcerting. Few people could hide their thoughts so completely. He would be a formidable adversary, she thought, feeling quite sorry for the people who would be facing him across the boardroom table, fighting for their company.

'Actually, I was simply passing the time until the heart attack breakfast arrives.' Then, with a small but unmistakably dismissive gesture, he said, 'It's called having a conversation.'

For once she regretted that her own personal drawbridge was quite so well-oiled. Regretted the conversation they might have had. Found it harder than usual to paint on the bright smile as she said, 'You don't have to be polite, Jude. I assumed this would be a working breakfast and brought my notebook with me.'

'Then you assumed wrong. This is just breakfast.'

'Oh,' she said, for a moment flummoxed. She'd anticipated eggs and dictation. 'Well, excellent. That means I can ask you to take a photograph of me with the pancakes and maple syrup.'

'Why on earth would you want a photograph of you eating breakfast?'

'Oh, please! Not eating it. Just looking at it.'

'Looking at your breakfast?' he persisted.

'It's a memory, Jude, that's all. I'll show my mother the picture, and then I'll tell her how everything tasted and how the waitress sounded and how rude you were and how rude I was, and of course she won't believe me—because, after all, who would?—and I'll grin and she'll say, "How lovely." And, "I wish I could have been there." And I'll say, "Pack your bags. I'll take you." And then she'll say, "Don't be silly…"' She stopped abruptly. Then, because he didn't say anything, and the silence desperately needed filling with inconsequential, meaningless chatter, 'Haven't you ever done that? Made a memory to share with someone?'

'Not my mother,' he said.

On the point of his asking her if she would be sharing it with anyone else the waitress returned with their breakfast, and Talie instantly engaged her in conversation. If he'd been a sensitive soul he'd have thought she was doing it to avoid talking to him, but her interest seemed genuine enough. That was Talie. What you saw was what you got. Even ordering a box of doughnuts to take out was an adventure to her. Should she have sprinkles, or jelly, or apple? He resisted the impulse to ask what she was going to do with them.

'So, we've established that you have a mother,' he persisted, when he'd finally reclaimed her attention. 'Is that the sum total of your family?'

'I have a younger brother, Liam. He's reading law at Edinburgh. You've just been to Scotland, haven't you? Walking?'

'I take a few days occasionally. To get away from people, telephones. The silence helps me to think.'

'About ways to make even more money?'

'You have a problem with that?'

'Surrounded by so much beauty…' she offered.

'There's nothing ugly about money. It's the lack of it that makes life difficult. A lot of people depend on me to pay their mortgages, keep their families fed and clothed.'

'You worry about them?'

'You're surprised?'

She shook her head. 'I'm sorry. No. I just hadn't considered it that way before. As a responsibility.'

'It's one I chose. I could sell up, walk away—but then what would I do with the rest of my life?'

'There are always new challenges.'

'That's why I need to think.'

'I didn't mean new ways to make money.'

She was very good at redirection, he thought. Steering the conversation away from topics she didn't want to talk about, pointing it back at him. Given the opportunity, most people would rather talk about themselves. Unfortunately for her, he wasn't most people.

Unfortunately for him, neither was she.

'Give me your camera and I'll take that picture now, so that your mother can see just what a gannet you are.'

'You think she doesn't already know that?' She took a small digital camera from her bag and said, 'You just look there to compose the picture and then press that button.'

'I think I can probably manage that.' He framed her in the small screen and for a moment felt the charge of her enthusiasm, her exuberance, coming straight at him. But there was something else, too, underlying the brightness. Something that if it wasn't so ridiculous he might have thought was loneliness. 'Smile…' he said, quite unnecessarily, pushing the unexpected tug of long-buried emotions firmly away. Then, 'Hold it for one more…'

He checked the pictures to make sure they were as flattering as a photograph of someone beaming over the breakfast could be, flicking through the ones she'd taken earlier at the same time. Yellow cabs, the stars and stripes hanging from a building, a mounted policeman, one of the Central Park buggies, views of the park itself. She had a good eye for a picture. A real pleasure in the new.

He envied her that. He couldn't remember the last time he'd gone somewhere he hadn't been a hundred times before. Seen something that had made him wish he had a camera so that he could capture the moment.

Even in Scotland it hadn't been the scenery that refreshed him. Just the silence.

'What about you, Talie?' he asked, returning her camera.

'What about me?'

'What do you think about?'

'"…*when the full moon is shining in…and the lamp is dying out…?*"'

'When you're sitting on the bus going to work was more what I had in mind. But if you're in a philosophical mood I'll indulge you.'

She didn't immediately respond, and he had the feeling that he had somehow missed his cue to change the subject. That she hadn't anticipated indulgence. 'On the other hand,' he said, picking up her discomfort, 'if that's just a polite way of saying "mind your own business…"'

'If you were being intrusive I wouldn't pussyfoot around. I'd tell you straight out.'

'Would you?'

Once again she was uncharacteristically silent.

How hard would he have to push before she ran out of those clever little diversionary tactics and got to the point where she was left with no choice but to talk or tell him to do just that?

Not that he needed to push. All he had to do was pick up a phone and he'd have her life history at his command. Where she lived. Where she went to school, college, her grades, everywhere she'd ever worked, every man she'd ever kissed. Perversely, he wanted her to trust him enough to tell him the important things herself. Especially why someone with her drive and skill—and a quick look through the work she'd produced before she left for her run was enough to demonstrate that she had both, in abundance—was working as a temp at an age when most educated women were already settled in a career, getting around to raising a family.

Why hadn't she mentioned sharing her memories with her father? Or any other man, for that matter.

But who was he to complain? He wasn't into sharing confidences either. All he needed to know was that she could do the job, and she'd already demonstrated that.

'Eat your breakfast, Talie,' he said. 'We haven't got all morning.'

'Of course. Time and take-overs wait for no man.'

They spent the rest of the morning dealing with e-mails from London before the UK office closed for the day, then refining the after-dinner speech he was to give that night. Then Talie summoned the car to take them downtown for a working lunch with the lawyers.

She was working hard to smother a yawn as she gathered her

notebook, checked her supply of pencils, and it occurred to him that she'd already put in a ten-hour day.

'I don't need you on this one,' he lied.

'Really?' Then, 'You're only saying that because you don't want me snoring through the meeting.'

'You snore?'

'You doubt it?'

He wasn't going there.

'Take a nap, Talie.'

'A nap? You think a nap will do it? I feel like going to bed and not getting up until tomorrow morning,' she said. 'In fact, I might do just that. You won't need me this evening, will you?'

'You're not planning on sleeping,' he said. 'You think you can get in some sightseeing while I'm putting my reputation on the line in front of five hundred bankers and stockbrokers.' He hadn't forgotten that late night phone call. Marcus knew Jude would be fully occupied this evening.

'There's no fooling you, is there?'

'And no point trying to. Besides, you're wrong about tonight. You don't think I'm going to sit through one of those boring business dinners without some prospect of entertainment, do you?'

'I'm sorry? Entertainment? Why would you need entertainment when you can talk about money all night?'

Which would teach him not to be smart mouthed at her expense.

'I'm sorry, Jude, on this occasion you are going to have to manage without your clown. Your totally efficient PA covered most things, but she didn't mention dress-up clothes and I haven't got anything remotely suitable to wear.'

He'd offended her, he realised. And for once she wasn't bothering to hide it behind a smile.

Maybe he'd meant to. She was much too distracting to be a PA. She could be the best in the business, but there was no way he was going to give her the job.

He found himself thinking about her instead of giving his full attention to the problem at hand. Found himself watching her quick, sure movements as she took notes, as her fingers flew over the keyboard without once looking at it. Seeing the bright intelligence that needed no second telling, no explanations... Waiting for the delighted smile that broke out at the slightest provocation. Catching the distant look that came into her eyes when she thought no one was looking.

She was getting under his skin, and he didn't allow that. But he wasn't giving Marcus the opportunity to get under hers.

'Clothes are not a problem,' he said. 'Buy something and charge it to me.'

Talie was feeling just the smallest bit miffed. She'd worked her socks off for Jude Radcliffe, producing immaculate work when anyone in their right mind would have been asleep.

She was entitled to an evening off.

But, no. He wanted company at the dinner tonight. She didn't object to that. If he'd said, Would you like to come? It's going to be about as much fun as watching paint dry and I'd really welcome the company of someone who makes me laugh…she wouldn't have turned him down.

How often did you get to have dinner with a millionaire, for heaven's sake? And not an old, crumpled one, but a tall, slate-eyed hunk of a millionaire who should, by rights, have a six-foot supermodel on his arm.

But she wasn't being asked. She was being commanded to dress up and provide him with 'entertainment.' And, unlike the rest of the guests, she didn't even have the keynote speech to look forward to. She already knew it practically by heart.

As if that wasn't bad enough, instead of taking a well-earned nap so that she wouldn't look like death by eight o'clock, she was going to have to shop for a dress. And she hadn't the first idea where to go.

Barney could have told her, but he'd taken Jude to his meeting. She could phone Heather. Maybe find out if *she* went along to these things. She should probably do that anyway and find out how things had gone with the baby. Jude would probably want to send flowers…

All she got was a message on the answering machine, telling her that the new arrival was a girl and everyone was doing well. Well, obviously she wouldn't be at home, but taking care of her daughter.

She would have left a message to say that they were doing pretty well in New York, too, but the tape was already full.

That left the hotel manager. She wasn't exactly thrilled at the prospect of asking the man for help, but the alternative was worse.

'Miss Calhoun,' he said, remembering her name without prompting, all smiles now he knew who she was. 'Please come through to the office.' And, when she was comfortably seated, 'How can I help you?'

'I'm looking for advice, Mr Luis. I joined Mr Radcliffe at very short notice, and now I discover he expects me to partner him at a business dinner this evening. Unfortunately I didn't pack anything suitable to wear.' She didn't actually possess anything remotely suitable to wear for partnering a millionaire—even as entertainment. 'I don't have a lot of time,' she said, 'and to be honest I don't even know where to begin.'

'If it's a business dinner I'd advise black.'

'The female equivalent of the dinner jacket? Isn't that a bit obvious?'

'On the contrary. On this kind of occasion "obvious" would be *not* wearing black. You need something elegant and understated,' he said, then regarded her, as if having trouble ratifying that description with reality.

'You don't think I can do understated?'

'On the contrary, Miss Calhoun. Having seen you reduce my security officers to quivering wrecks, I'm certain you can do anything you put your mind to.'

They were quivering wrecks!

'I did apologise.'

'I know. And you took them a box of doughnuts, too. They would probably die for you now.'

'Really—that won't be necessary.'

'Let us hope so. Now, if you'll just let me make one phone call…'

Within minutes he had arranged for her to see a personal shopper at a seriously up-market department store, and for her purchases to be charged to Jude Radcliffe's account with the hotel.

'If you have any problems, just call me,' he said, giving her his card.

'Thank you, Mr Luis.'

'It's my pleasure, Miss Calhoun. Is there anything else I can do for you?'

'Well, if "understated" is the order of the day, I should probably have my hair put in restraints.'

'There's a salon in the hotel. I'll let them know you'll need some time later in the afternoon. Just go along there when you're ready.'

The store was near enough to walk to, and by the time she'd arrived her Personal Shopper, who was tall, scarily elegant and understated to the point of invisibility, had a selection of dresses, shoes and accessories waiting for her to try on.

Understatement could grow on her, Talie decided, flicking through a dozen or so exquisitely cut black dresses.

Although one wouldn't want to overdo it.

'Jude?'

He was having a bad meeting. It wasn't that anything was going wrong; on the contrary, everything was going precisely to plan. His invitation to speak at the annual bankers' dinner had been the perfect cover for his trip to the U.S., and there hadn't been the slightest hint of the proposed take-over in the press on either side of the Atlantic.

He was, however, finding it difficult to give his undivided attention to the agenda.

Guilt, unexpectedly, was nagging at him. Heaven alone knew what had possessed him to insist Talie accompany him to the dinner. He would never have asked Heather to join him, and if he had she'd have known he was joking. Except that this time he hadn't been...

'Jude?'

He realised that Marcus was waiting for a response from him and was forced to mentally scroll back through the previous conversation before he could provide it.

CHAPTER SIX

TALIE slept through her facial and manicure, and still had time for an hour with a cucumber compress over her eyes before the telephone rang to wake her with the alarm call she'd booked.

She replaced the receiver, then lay back against the pillow, a hand over her stomach to quiet the little thrill of anticipation that fluttered through her. Buffed, polished, and with the most expensive dress she'd ever possessed hanging in the wardrobe, she had long forgotten her irritation at having to forgo an evening sightseeing.

She didn't even care that Jude hadn't thought it necessary to ask, rather than command.

She was excited, she realised. And just a bit nervous. The way she'd used to feel before going out on a big date. She could just about remember how that felt. Not that she'd ever been out on a date with a man like Jude Radcliffe.

She wasn't now, she reminded herself, firmly rejecting all thoughts of the way he'd held her hand when she was gibbering unattractively with nervousness as their flight left the ground, the touch of his fingers against her cheek as he'd tucked a stray curl behind her ear.

It wasn't personal. Her hair annoyed him, that was all. Hell, it annoyed her...

This was just a work thing. Obviously Jude needed someone along to take care of his speech, hand it to him at the appropriate moment...

No. That wasn't it. He was more than capable of taking care of his own speech. She couldn't think why he needed her with him, but being seen in the company of one of the world's most powerful businessmen was undoubtedly going to be the highlight of her year.

Probably her entire decade, the way things were going.

What it was going to be for him, she wasn't sure, but he undoubtedly had some good reason for wanting her there, and she doubted that it had anything to do with 'entertainment.'

If it was, he was going to be disappointed. She was going to be his Girl Friday. Supportive, discreet, doing absolutely nothing to draw attention to herself. Doing absolutely nothing that would give his eyebrow an excuse to get excited.

This was a once-in-a-lifetime Cinderella moment, and she wasn't going to do a thing to wreck it. She was going to be the perfect young businesswoman. Make him eat his 'entertainment' if it killed her.

She glanced at her watch. Plenty of time. And she smiled as she imagined his face as she walked into the room. Stunned by the elegant and understated perfection of her dress. Bowled over by her sleek new hairstyle.

'Talie…' He'd murmur her name on little more than a breath as he reached for her hand, whispered her name again, as if he could hardly believe his eyes as he bent to kiss her cheek and she caught the subtle scent of an Alpha male for once lost for words.

'Talie, you look…'

'Talie!'

She sat up with a start.

'Talie, are you ready?'

What? Ready? She looked at her watch.

Oh, sugar… She'd gone straight back to sleep.

'Ten minutes,' she mumbled, tumbling off the bed, trying to get her mouth to cooperate with her brain and her feet to go in the same direction as she scrambled for the bathroom.

Oh, good grief! Ten minutes wasn't long enough to be stunning. Ten minutes was barely long enough to be herself. She groaned. That would teach her to go daydreaming about laying waste to tall, dark and handsome millionaires.

And even if he did fall at her feet she'd just have to tell him to get up again. This Cinderella wasn't in the market for a prince—Charming or otherwise.

It was just as well that she hadn't planned on a leisurely shower—the steam would have reduced her carefully straightened hair to ringlets—since all she had time for was the shortest sponge down in history. With cold water.

And since, for once, she didn't have to do anything to her hair except flatten it with a brush where it was sticking up after she'd slept on it, she had absolutely loads of time to spend on her makeup—three whole minutes, in fact—before she slipped into the slither of silk crêpe that had probably cost more per square inch than anything she'd ever worn. Or was ever likely to.

Fortunately, since 'understated' people didn't discuss the price of anything, she'd never know exactly how much. And by the time the bill arrived on Jude's desk she'd be ancient history.

Ditto her new shoes and evening bag.

Jude was on the telephone when the door behind him opened, and he glanced at his wristwatch. Ten minutes dead. The girl was good, he thought, turning around. And he discovered to his surprise that breathing was not the simple, automatic thing that he'd always imagined it to be.

'Jude…?' The voice in his ear demanded a response. 'Are you there?'

'Yes—sorry, someone just came in…' And for the second time that day he found himself having to re-run a conversation before he could respond. Except that on this occasion his mind was a total blank. 'Let's talk about this tomorrow, Mike,' he said. 'I'm on my way out.'

'I'm sorry,' Talie said, with a tiny gesture towards the phone as he replaced the receiver. 'I didn't mean to disturb you.'

Didn't she? Then why the devil was she wearing a dress clearly designed for the purpose of disturbing any man with half a red blood cell? Although how just one bare shoulder, one bare arm, could be so…provocative was beyond him.

It wasn't as if the dress was tight. Or clinging. On the contrary, it skimmed her figure, merely hinting at the curves he knew it concealed. Maybe that was it. Concealment. And the counter-point of creamy white skin against unrelieved black.

After his remark about 'entertainment' he'd steeled himself for something outrageous in scarlet. With frills. He knew he deserved it.

Subtle, he discovered, could be far more deadly. If he'd wanted her to cause a distraction he'd got everything he could have wished for.

Of course it didn't help that as she walked towards him the curved hem parted to the thigh to offer a glimpse of strappy shoe with a heel high enough to be used as a lethal weapon, a slender ankle, and just enough shapely leg to lay waste any banker whose arteries were not in tiptop condition.

His own heart was pounding uncomfortably, and he was familiar with her legs. He'd had a close up of them that morning, when she was wearing her running shorts.

Less, he decided, was definitely more.

She stopped. The skirt became still. Discreet. And he managed to drag his gaze back to her face.

'What the hell have you done with your hair?' he asked. He had to say something, and, on balance, her hair seemed safest. Gone were the wild curls. It was hanging sleek and straight to her shoulders, with just the tiniest lift at the ends.

He'd asked for it. And he discovered that he hated it.

'Nothing. I—and when I say I, I do, of course, mean you—paid a hairdresser a vast amount of money to iron it straight. I'm afraid you've had a rather expensive afternoon all 'round. But there it is.' And she gave a little shrug that offered him another glimpse of her ankle. 'High-quality entertainment doesn't come cheap.'

'We should be leaving,' he said.

'I'm ready.' Then, 'Don't forget your speech.' She picked up the stack of prompt cards from the desk and handed them to him. She used the sleeveless arm—it didn't even have a bracelet to make it look less naked—and taking them from her fingers felt like sin.

He slipped them into his pocket before opening the door and standing well back to allow her to precede him. He couldn't think of a thing to say as they rode down together in the lift, and Talie, for once silent, didn't help him out. But as they made their way through the lobby he couldn't miss the ripple of turning heads, the murmur of interest as, placing himself carefully on her sleeved side, he guided her to the door.

It was opened by Mr Luis himself, with the smallest bow to Talie. But it was left to Barney to say what everyone was thinking.

'Wow, Talie. Great dress. You look fabulous.'

'Thank you, Barney,' she said, smiling at him as she ducked her head, her hair swinging forward as she climbed into the back of the car.

He should have said it, he knew, but it was too late. Anything he said now was simply going to echo the quiet nod from the hotel manager, Barney's natural spontaneity.

And look second-hand.

He was stuck with a throw-away line about 'entertainment.'

'Mr Radcliffe…'

He paused at the entrance to the hotel where the dinner was being held and their arrival was met by a barrage of flashes from photographers taking pictures for the financial papers.

'Okay?' he asked, glancing down at Talie.

'Oh, yes. Just a bit surprised. I didn't expect the celebrity treatment.'

'Why not? You look like a star.'

Maybe that was the way to do it. Just say what you were thinking—without thinking about it. How long had it been since he'd done that?

He discovered he could pinpoint the exact day, hour, minute…

It was perhaps as well that they were instantly swept up by the reception committee and he didn't have to follow up his remark with the usual crushing put-down. Instead he could much more safely introduce her to their host.

So much for dreaming, Talie thought as she was offered a glass of champagne. One brief glance and a 'What the hell have you done with your hair…?' She was beginning to think the girls in the Finance Department at the Radcliffe Tower were right. The man was a total…

'Is this your first visit to New York, Talie?'

The men were older, more powerful, but the questions, the exclamations over her accent, the invitations were the same. Unfortunately the only man she wanted to invite her to go sight-seeing had other things on his mind. When Jude was asked by one of the party if he could spare her to sit by him at dinner, so that they could 'talk about London,' he was too busy talking about his favourite subject to do more than glance up and frown, as if he'd forgotten all about her, before, after a momentary pause during which she thought he was going to decline—she was there for *his* 'entertainment' after all—he nodded.

She bottled up her disappointment, hiding it beneath a smile, hoping she looked as if he'd done her a favour.

As if he'd notice.

Cool, elegant, sophisticated, she reminded herself, and once they were seated she turned to the man who'd sought out her company. 'So, when were you last in London, Carson?' she asked, doing her best to ignore Jude. He didn't seem to be having any trouble ignoring her.

Carson needed little prompting to talk about himself, and she gave him her full attention for a while before turning to the man on her left and sitting through an almost identical conversation. Getting on first name terms with millionaires was getting to be a habit, but it wasn't so difficult. They were just like other men.

Most of them.

Jude hoped that putting some distance between him and Talie would help. It didn't. Instead of having her next to him where, though he'd be assaulted by her voice, her scent, the certainty that every man's eye was upon her, he wouldn't have to look at her, he was now sitting opposite her and forced to watch every move, every smile, every laugh as she captivated the men sitting around her.

She wasn't just a runaway chatterbox, he discovered. She knew how to listen, and it wasn't only young, impressionable men who vied for her attention.

Old, impressionable men were equally Talie-struck.

He couldn't even justify his irritation by pretending that she was flirting outrageously with them. She wasn't. She didn't need to flirt. All she had to do was smile and they were at her feet—and once again falling over themselves to provide a personalised tour of the city.

'Carson, I allowed you the pleasure of Talie's company over dinner, but don't push your luck,' he warned.

'You can't blame an old man for trying.'

'It's becoming an epidemic. Men all over New York take one look at Talie and instantly decide they must take her "sightseeing." It never happens when I bring Heather with me.'

'Heather is a lovely woman. I promise next time she comes to New York I'll take her wherever she'd like to go.' The old man grinned. 'But only if I get Talie tomorrow.'

'Really, I don't have time for sightseeing, Carson,' she said quickly. 'I'm here to work.'

'You must have some time to yourself. Just because Jude thinks the world revolves around the office doesn't mean you have to subscribe to the same philosophy. All work and no play—'

'Makes a man dull, but rich,' Jude cut in. 'Spare me your homespun philosophy, Carson, especially since you've never adhered to it yourself. How many wives have given up on you?'

'Four.'

'I thought it was five.'

Carson appeared to think about it. 'You're right. Five. But given sufficient incentive a man can change.'

'In this case he isn't going to get the chance. Didn't Talie tell you that I'm taking her on a night-time tour of the city just as soon as we leave here?' He turned to her. 'Tell him, Talie.'

'That's right. Beginning with a visit to the top of the Empire State Building,' she responded without hesitation, smiling across the table at him. Familiar with the entire range of her smiles by now, he was not fooled for a minute. She was not in the least bit amused. 'It's so much more romantic at night. Isn't that right, Jude?' she prompted.

Romantic? Oh, good grief…

'That remains to be seen,' he replied. 'I believe the forecast is for rain.'

CHAPTER SEVEN

TALIE was not impressed.

'What was that all about?' she demanded as they left the hotel, the minute his speech was over, the applause still ringing in their ears.

'What didn't you understand? I thought you had a pretty sound grasp of economics,' he replied, as Barney opened the limo door for her to climb in.

'For a woman?'

'Don't be petty, Talie. It doesn't suit you.'

'No. Sorry. Anyway, I wasn't talking about the speech, as well you know. I already knew that by heart.'

Not entirely true. She knew the words by heart, but he'd put life, passion into them, given them power and meaning. And humour. He'd had them all laughing at the stories with which he'd interspersed his hard-news message on the economy. It had been a world away from reading the words off a computer screen or the prompt cards she'd prepared—and which he'd barely glanced at.

He'd engaged with his audience on a personal level that had surprised and warmed her. She'd felt, somehow, that he was talking directly to her. And she suspected that everyone else in the room had felt the same way.

'It was excellent, by the way.'

'I'd say I'm flattered, although I sense a lurking "but…"'

'If there is it's a butt with two ts,' she said. 'There was no need for you to butt into my conversation with Carson. I wasn't about to spill the beans—tell him I was too busy to go sightseeing because my boss needed me to hold his hand while he takes over yet another company.' Then, when he didn't rise to this provocation, 'Even though he did offer to take me on a boat ride around Manhattan.'

'You need someone to take you to the pier? Buy your ticket? I thought you were a modern woman who didn't need a man to hold her hand.'

'I don't. Carson was offering to take me in his yacht.'

'Really? I thought wife number five had got that in the divorce settlement.'

'Don't be petty, Jude.'

'No. I'm sorry to have spoiled your fun.'

'I didn't want to go with him,' she declared furiously. 'I'm not cross because you interfered with my social life. We both know that I don't have time to go pleasure cruising. But if you didn't think I could be trusted to keep my mouth shut why did you take me with you tonight?'

'It never occurred to me that you'd talk about my business dealings over the dinner table, Talie. Heather chose you. I trust her judgement.'

Slightly mollified, she said, 'Well, good. But you're lucky I'm not the kind of girl to hold a man to the promise of a good time.'

'Are you telling me you're too tired?' he asked.

'What?' Then, 'No, but you didn't mean it…'

'I never say anything I don't mean. Give us your New York By Night Special, Barney. Starting at 350 Fifth Avenue. Talie wants to take a long ride in an elevator.'

'Yes, sir!'

'You did mean it?' she said, her heart picking up a beat as he slid onto the seat beside her.

He shrugged, drawing attention to the kind of shoulders that would have looked more at home on an athlete than a businessman. She'd been trying to ignore them all evening. Trying to ignore him the way he'd been ignoring her. The amount of attention she'd paid him, it was scarcely any wonder that Carson had thought it was his lucky night…

'I was looking for a believable excuse to leave early,' he said. 'Before the heavy talking starts. You gave me one.'

'So that's why you took me along.' She gestured back towards the hotel as the car pulled away from the kerb. 'They all think "sightseeing" is a euphemism for the shortest route to the bedroom.'

'I don't suppose for a minute any of them thought I'd brought you to New York for your shorthand skills, Talie. Not in that dress.'

'What's wrong with the dress?' she demanded. 'I went for elegant and understated, which was a good deal more than you deserved. I could have gone for seriously "entertaining,"' she reminded him, making little quote marks with her fingers. 'With a hemline up to here and a neckline down to here and—'

'And caused a riot?'

'Men are so shallow,' she said, trying very hard not to smile.

'Are we? So, who do you sleep with?'

Which would teach her to try and be smart with a man who'd forgotten more about manipulating conversation than she'd ever known. Teach her to use a cheap trick to stop the conversation when it was getting too personal. Jude had simply stored it away, using it back at her after he'd slipped beneath her defences with a compliment. But she rallied gamely.

'Do I have to be sleeping with anyone? It isn't compulsory, as far as I know.'

'I've seen the effect you have on the average male libido—' she didn't miss the 'average,' something they both knew he was not '—so unless all the men in London are blind or idiots, it follows that you must be beating them off in droves.'

'I wish. It's just the English accent exciting the locals. It doesn't have the same effect at home. And I think you lend me a little of your glamour, Jude. You must have noticed that a girl arriving in the wake of a millionaire becomes instantly more interesting.'

'So the answer is no one?'

This time he wasn't going to allow himself to be diverted, and confined with him in the rear of a limousine there was no escape—short of doing what she'd said she'd do and telling him to mind his own business. Which would put a swift end to the evening. Something that she didn't want. And not just because he'd promised her that long ride in a lift.

Why was it that 'no one' sounded so lame? It wasn't as if it was from lack of offers. It was her choice, and Jude didn't care one way or the other. He was just satisfying his curiosity. Demonstrating his power.

It didn't matter, she told herself.

Oh, but it did. Somehow admitting that the only male who ever spent the night beneath her duvet these days was Harry, the little stray black and white cat who'd invited himself in and made himself at home, was not the image she was hoping to project in her sexy black dress. A girl had her pride.

She could, of course, invent an intense and adoring lover, but it was late, and she knew she wouldn't remember what she'd said in the morning. And she'd already left it far too long to be convincing.

'It's late, Jude. If we're going to do "conversation," can we stick to simple stuff? I need a full eight hours' sleep before I can deal with advanced level.'

'If you need time to think about it, Talie, don't stress yourself. I can work it out for myself.'

Now she felt like a fool. She should have owned up to the cat…and the teddy. Her turn to shrug. 'Okay, I'll admit it. I'm a sad old bag who's on the shelf.'

'There are several things wrong with that statement, but they'll have to wait.' And, while she was still trying to work that one out, 'We've arrived,' he said. 'Do you want to do this, or would you rather go to bed?'

Startled, she turned to look at him. In the darkness of the limousine his eyes gleamed dangerously, and every cell in her body responded with shocking immediacy. 'Go to bed?' she repeated.

Oh, great, Talie. Come and out and say it, why don't you? After all, you're only his temporary secretary, and everyone already assumes you're sleeping with him. Why not give yourself a real treat? You know you want to…

'And put in a bid for the eight hours' sleep.'

'Oh…' For once entirely lost for words, she turned and glanced out of the car window. Then, as she saw the address—understated and elegant in art deco script—she said it again. 'Oh… Wow!' At least she didn't have to pretend enthusiasm in an attempt to hide her blushes. 'We're really here.'

'I'll take that as a vote for the ride in a lift.'

Jude climbed out and offered her his hand. Taking it, she allowed him to lead her into the entrance, but dug her heels in when he walked straight past the exquisite 1930s lift lobby.

'Where are we going?'

'I'm afraid the paying public don't get to use that area. Three and a half million people a year require something a little more hard-wearing. We go down here.'

'We do?' Then, seeing the signs, 'We have to queue?'

'I'm afraid so. Although it's late, so hopefully not for long.'

There was a photographer waiting to snap arrivals in front of a backdrop of the building.

'You don't have to buy if you don't like it,' he said, when Talie hesitated.

'Oh, right.'

'You want me to take you together?'

'No.' She quickly detached herself from Jude before he took the initiative and did it for her. 'Just me.'

'Number eleven. You can pick it up on the way out,' he said.

'It wasn't like this in *Sleepless in Seattle*,' Talie said as Jude headed towards the window to pay. For once she had to think of something to say to fill the void, rather than just letting the words spill out.

'You should get out more. This is real life, not a movie, Talie.' He took her by the arm and led her towards the lifts. 'At least it's fairly quiet. At midday this place is heaving.'

'I see. Obviously you've been here before. Despite the fervent protestations to the contrary, it would seem that you're not entirely immune to sightseeing.'

'No, I've done my share. But after a while it all gets to look the same, so now I just concentrate on business.'

'You're just a cynical old man who's seen it all. Maybe you should wait in the car. Or go back to the hotel and work on a deal. I can get a taxi back to the hotel. I haven't been in a yellow cab yet and it would give me a chance to tick it off my to-do list.'

It occurred to her that she was beginning to sound crabby—unrequited lust had that effect on her—and she shut her mouth.

'You'll need someone to take a photograph of you at the top

to prove you've been there, won't you?' He took the small bag she was carrying from her. 'Or are you going to pretend that you didn't bring your camera with you, just to prove me wrong?'

'You are such a know-all,' she declared, snatching it back before he could look.

'Not at all. The enthusiastic tourist never travels without her camera—or how would she remember everything she's seen?'

'I'll never forget what I've seen. The photographs aren't for me—'

'I know. They're for your mother. I'm beginning to wish you'd brought her with you. She could have taken her own photographs while you concentrated on work.'

She stared at him. She was entitled to be a little crabby. He was the man of her dreams as well as being the boss from hell. It was a very bad combination. But this outing was his idea, so what was *his* problem?

Then the lift arrived and she let the bad feelings go, taking a deep breath as she stepped inside.

As they joined the dozen or so other people who'd been waiting, and rode up in unnatural silence, Jude was unable to take his eyes off her. Wide-eyed and holding her breath, she watched the floor numbers being counted in tens as the high-speed lift sped them to the top, and despite himself he found her excitement infectious.

A second lift took them the last few floors, and he pushed open the door to the viewing platform, holding it wide so that she had an uninterrupted view of the city lit up before them.

'Oh.' She took a step down, then another. 'Oh, my goodness, it's so beautiful,' she said, her voice catching in her throat. Then she looked back up at him. 'Thank you, Jude.'

'Don't waste your time thanking me,' he said, his own voice catching just a little as her hair whipped across her face in the breeze. 'Go and take your pictures.'

He followed as she walked slowly around the viewing deck, stopping from time to time to exclaim at some spectacular sight…a bridge, a building she recognised, a name.

'Hey, there's Macy's! Right down there, below us.'

He looked down, then at her. 'Yes. So?'

'It's *Macy's*. The department store.'

'It's too late to go shopping.'

'No…it's on 34th Street,' she said, as if that should mean something to him.

'This has something to do with a movie, doesn't it?'

She stared at him. 'I can't believe you haven't seen *Miracle on…*' She stopped. 'No, I'm not wasting another breath talking to an old cynic like you. I doubt you ever believed in Santa Claus.'

'I am not old,' he protested, putting twenty-five cents in the binoculars for her so that she could look at the distant lights. 'I'm like the street. Thirty-four. In my prime.'

'Really?' She looked through the glasses, moving them until she found something that caught her attention. 'Cynicism is sooo aging.'

'You see wrinkles? Grey hair?' he demanded.

'That's just time showing, not age. Age isn't anything to do with muscle tone. It's in the mind.'

'Are you suggesting that I have a grey, sagging mind?' Then, when she actually looked as if she was giving it some thought, 'Hesitate one second more and you're fired.'

'You can't fire me. The enthusiastic tycoon needs his Girl Friday to keep track of his thoughts. However grey.' Then she smiled. 'Fortunately the condition is not incurable. Do want to take a look at the Statue of Liberty?' she asked, standing back and offering him the glasses.

'I've seen it, thanks.'

She tutted, catching her hair and tucking it behind her ear before taking another look for herself. 'On the other hand, some cases are beyond help.'

'Oh, I see. That was a test?'

'The view is always new, Jude.'

'Really? And what bumper sticker did you read that on?'

She didn't answer, just stepped back, shivered a little as she looked around, and rubbed her arms. He took off his jacket and slipped it around her shoulders, pulling it close in front of her. As she looked up to thank him he saw the lights of Manhattan reflected in her eyes and discovered that she was right. Even the most familiar scene in the world could take on a totally new dimension if he took the trouble to look.

'Is that it?' he said, fighting down the urge to kiss her that had been dogging him ever since she'd looked up at him in his own lift. 'Have you finally run out of snappy little homilies?'

'You have to *want* to be rescued, Jude.'

Rescued?

'I'm not lost.'

'You're just in denial. What you need is a twelve-step plan to recover your sense of wonder.'

'Wonder?' Was that what he saw in her eyes? The excitement that seemed to radiate from her and light up any room? 'Okay, I'll let that pass on the grounds that you're suffering from jet lag.'

'Step one is admitting you have a problem.'

'The only problem I have is you, Talie Calhoun. Give me your camera and I'll take a photograph of you.'

For a moment the image in her eyes seemed to shimmer, then she lowered her lashes as she opened her bag to take out her camera and the image was gone. By the time she looked up her smile seemed to have lost its natural sparkle and become mechanical.

'Talie—'

'Do you want me to take a photograph of the two of you together?'

Before Talie could say it wasn't necessary Jude had handed the camera to the kindly woman who'd offered. 'That would be great. Thank you.'

And, after glancing down, he scooped Talie under his arm and lined her up for the shot. 'If we stand here,' he said, 'you'll be able to tell your mother that Macy's is right behind us.'

She muttered something under her breath that he didn't quite catch—wasn't meant to catch. He thought it wiser not to ask her to repeat it.

'One more to be sure?' the woman asked.

'Thank you,' Talie said, sliding out from under his arm and reclaiming the camera immediately the woman had taken the second photograph, tucking it straight into her bag without looking at them.

'A pleasure. You two have a nice evening.'

'Shall we take a rain check on the rest of the tour, Jude?' Talie said, turning to him. 'It's getting late and we've got a busy day tomorrow.'

He glanced back at the city, sparkling with light, colour, and felt an odd reluctance to leave. But Talie was already heading towards the exit and he followed her, catching her in time to open the door.

'You're tired?'

'I'll survive. At least I will if I don't wake up at three o'clock again.'

'If you do, give me a knock and we could have a crack at some of that advanced conversation. The wee small hours of the morning are supposed to be conducive to the spilling of secrets.'

'Who said I have secrets?'

'Everyone has secrets, Talie, and you're already privy to a lot of mine.'

'Business secrets don't count.'

'No?'

'No.' She managed a grin. 'So if we're going to share pre-dawn confidences you're going to have to be prepared to trade.'

CHAPTER EIGHT

TALIE opened her eyes and thought for a moment that she'd overslept. Then she picked up her watch and fell back against the pillows. Four o'clock. A marginal improvement on the previous night, but not by much, and while her head was telling her to close her eyes and go back to sleep her body was wide awake, eager to leap out of bed and go for an early-morning run.

That was the trouble with habits, they died hard, but there hadn't been a lot to stay in bed for in the last couple of years, and lying there feeling sorry for herself hadn't been an attractive option.

She hadn't even given it more than a passing thought for quite some time—there was no use pining over what you couldn't have—until she'd been blindsided by a good looking stranger in a lift and had found herself remembering just what she'd been missing.

She turned over, buried her head under the pillow and tried to block out the promptings of a body kept on short rations for too long—a body suddenly confronted with all the temptations in the sweet shop window and demanding gratification.

There had been a moment, the space of one slow heartbeat, when Jude had put his jacket around her and she'd been certain that he was about to make an unforgettable memory just for her, up there on top of the world—the kind that no camera could compete with. But a kiss wouldn't have been enough.

And anything more would have been impossible.

It didn't stop her thinking about it, though.

She could have done with a pile of work to attack and fill the empty hours until dawn. She didn't even have a book or a

magazine to distract her. She might have been a bit slow to work
out who he was, but once she'd got the picture she'd understood
that asking him to wait while she grabbed the latest bestseller as
they flashed through the airport shopping mall would not go
down at all well.

She turned the pillow over to the cool side, lay very still, and
used basic relaxation techniques to make her limbs go heavy,
doing her best to ignore the time-to-get-up insistence of a body
used to routine. It was no good. All that happened was that she
was relaxed and wide awake.

She eased herself into a sitting position, picked up the phone
and dialled home, where it was a civilised nine o'clock in the
morning. Her aunt answered.

'Talie? What time is it with you?'

'Don't ask. I can't sleep and it's too early to get up. Can you
call me back for a chat?' she begged—she'd given her aunt her
number at the hotel so that she wouldn't have to pay for her calls
home at hotel rates—and snatched the phone back up the minute
it began to ring.

Jude, unable to sleep, heard the brief ring of the phone and
glanced at his watch. It was just past four. An odd time for a
phone call—unless it was from home. And, concerned that it
might be bad news, he flung back the covers and pulled on a robe
before crossing the sitting room to Talie's room.

He tapped. The low murmur of her voice stopped, then she
said, 'Yes?'

Taking that as an invitation, he opened the door.

Talie was sitting propped up against a pile of pillows in the
huge bed, her eyes dark and lustrous in a dim circle of light
from the bedside lamp. Her hair had given up on the expensive
styling and curled back into its natural ringlets and she was
wearing what looked like a baggy T-shirt with a cartoon
kangaroo printed on the front.

As an essay in seduction it should have been a disaster. His
body was quick to tell him that it was anything but. He'd never
seen a woman looking so appealing, so desirable, so sexy...

'What is it, Jude?' she demanded.

Jerked out of the fantasy his mind was weaving, he said, 'I heard the phone. Is anything wrong?'

'No. I couldn't sleep, so I asked my aunt to call me for a chat.'

'Hang up. Talk to me; it's cheaper.'

'You're not paying for the call,' she objected.

'All the more reason to do as I say and stop squandering your hard earned money. I'll go and make a cup of tea,' he said.

And he tore himself away before he forgot himself…and the fact that she worked for him. Busying himself filling the kettle, finding the tea bags, he tried not to think of how it would feel to have her warm body curled up against him, her hair soft beneath his hand…

'I'm sorry I disturbed you—'

He fumbled a mug as he dropped a tea bag into it, juggling with it until he finally managed to set it straight on the counter before he looked around.

'That's a bad case of nerves,' she said, going through the cupboards. 'You really should try to get more sleep.'

The kangaroo had been hidden beneath one of the thick white bathrobes provided by the hotel, and she looked as soft and cuddly as a teddy bear and ten times more appealing. She found what she was looking for—a teapot—and when she straightened they were standing very close.

She smelled of clean sheets, soap and warm skin. Innocent scents that stirred him in a way that the most expensive perfume never could. And unless he moved she was going to have to squeeze by him.

He didn't move.

For a moment the only thing that moved in the kitchen was his heart, beating as if he'd been hitting the treadmill in the basement gym instead of lying in bed for the last few hours.

She was so still that for a moment he thought she must be able to read his mind. Then she handed him the pot and said, 'Warm this, will you? If we're going to have tea it might as well be a decent cup.'

'Yes, ma'am.' His voice was throaty, his hand not quite steady as he poured in some water from the kettle, then swished it around before tipping it into the sink. 'So, you ring home and ask them to call you back?' he said stupidly.

It would explain the phone calls—although they must be keeping somewhat extended hours back home.

Her aunt?

'It's a lot cheaper than paying inflated hotel rates,' she said.

'I wouldn't expect you to pay for your calls home,' he said, angry with himself for not having thought to tell her so. 'Besides, the lines to the suite are private. Nothing to do with the hotel. Call whenever you want to.'

'Thank you. That's very kind.'

'No, it's totally selfish. I want your entire attention on the job, not worrying about what's going on at home. And you didn't disturb me. I was awake.'

She fished the tea bags out of the mugs and, taking the teapot from him, dropped them in before pouring on boiling water. 'Milk or lemon?'

'Milk.'

She raised her eyebrows. 'You've got the fridge.'

Obviously she wasn't prepared to squeeze by and get it herself.

Pity. There was something so intimate about sharing a kitchen in the middle of the night. The air was pregnant with possibilities. Loaded with risk.

He was no stranger to financial risk, but it was so long since he'd played roulette with his emotions that he'd forgotten the urgency, the complete abandonment of all sense—the single-minded need to plunge into danger.

She carefully poured the tea.

He topped it up with milk.

'Thanks,' she said, reaching for a mug.

Forestalling her before she could take it up and escape back to the safety of her bedroom, he picked up both of them. 'Let's go and sit down.'

'There must be a better way to do this,' she said, curling up in the armchair. It was a big armchair, but the message was plain. She was determined to keep her distance. So he took the sofa.

'Better way to do what?'

'Travel.' She took a sip of tea. 'They knew how to do it in the old days. Six days of luxury on an ocean liner. And no jet lag.'

'There's no reason why we shouldn't do that next time.' *We? Next time?* Where had that come from? He didn't actually care, he decided. The idea was intensely appealing. 'Ease ourselves gradually into the change of time zone by an hour a day. Arrive fresh and completely in tune with our surroundings.'

'Six days? Can you spare that much time?' she asked, refusing to pick up on the 'we.'

'I could give up walking in the Highlands. I imagine I would think just as well walking around the deck.'

'Well, obviously the scenery doesn't mean a thing to you, but you fly to New York a lot oftener than you take those breaks. I've seen your diary,' she said, when he raised his eyebrows. 'And I doubt you'd find an Atlantic crossing anywhere near as peaceful. There are all those cocktail parties, for a start.' She tapped her hand to her mouth in a parody of a bored yawn. 'The daily intake of dry martinis would lay waste to at least a zillion brain cells.'

He laughed. 'Would that be so bad? Since I only use them to think about money?'

'You might want to use them for something else one day.'

'What *is* your problem with money?'

'I don't have a problem with it. As you say, your staff have mortgages to pay, shoes to buy for their children. I'm glad you take your responsibilities seriously. I just think that there comes a time in a man's life when he should stop giving his entire attention to making the stuff and start thinking about how to use it.'

'For the good of mankind?'

'What else is it for?'

Caught without a slick answer, he said, 'Shall we get back to the important business of crossing the Atlantic without jet lag?'

'If you insist.' She shrugged, but he was sure she hadn't finished with that one. 'Where were we? Oh, right. The nightly cocktail party—followed, of course, by dinner at the Captain's table—'

'You think we'd get an invitation?'

'I don't know about "we." This has nothing to do with me. But a man with a whole building named after him could expect nothing less,' she declared.

'To be strictly accurate, it was named after my father.'

'He built it?'

'No. He died in an industrial accident when I was four years old. I built it and named it for him. The John Radcliffe Tower.'

'I'm sorry, I didn't know.'

'It's on the foundation stone. I'll show you when we get back.'

'Oh, but—'

'Do you think there would be deck games?' he prompted, refusing to allow her to spoil the fantasy by reminding him of the grinding poverty he'd come from. Or that she wouldn't be there when they got back.

'I should imagine so.' She pulled a face. Then, 'Don't they have shooting contests? Using those clay things? Very noisy.'

'They're big boats. We could find somewhere quiet. Sit out on the deck and watch the waves go by.'

'This is the Atlantic we're talking about, Jude. Force five gales and waves as big as… Well, I don't know how big they are, but they're bound to be really big.'

'You seem to know all about it.'

'I read a travel brochure once.'

'One that mentioned force five gales?'

'Well, no. It just said something about the boat being fitted with stabilisers and I read between the lines. I mean, why would a boat need stabilisers if there weren't big waves?'

'You didn't book a cruise, I take it?'

'It wasn't for me…' She shook her head. 'Look, I promise you, a man who's seen everything and done everything would be bored witless in six minutes, let alone six days. I mean, the Atlantic looks the same all the way across.'

'I'm willing to make the sacrifice if you are.'

'Aren't you forgetting something? I'm just a temp. Heather Lester is your secretary. She's a fine woman. The perfect PA.'

He wasn't forgetting a thing.

'Perfect, but no longer a fixture. She's been talking about retiring as soon as I can find someone to replace her. In fact she gave me twelve months' notice. It'll soon be up.'

'Have you found anyone?'

'I haven't been looking. I was counting on her changing her

mind. Now I suspect that she's done it for me. And she's chosen you.'

'Then she's going to be stuck with you for a while longer. I can't take on that kind of commitment. Did I tell you that her daughter had a little girl, by the way? Would you like me to send flowers? I would have done it, but I didn't know her daughter's married name. Or address.'

'Congratulations, Talie.'

A small frown creased the smooth skin between her brows.

'You managed to stay with the same conversation for all of fifteen minutes. Of course it was all pure fantasy. No real life stuff to send you running for cover. But the minute it got personal you changed the subject.'

'No, honestly—'

'Why can't you take on the kind of commitment that working for me would entail?'

There was a long pause. She looked into the mug of tea she was holding, as if that would offer her an escape.

'I'm sure Heather knows,' he prompted. 'She wouldn't have considered sending you on this trip unless she'd already thoroughly checked you out. Something I know she's done. She even checked out your story about the incident on the Underground.'

'That's outrageous! Why would I have lied about that?' Then, as her quick brain answered her own question, a flush stole across her cheeks. 'Oh. I see. You thought I'd made it up to impress you. That I was coming on to you.'

'Actually, no. But Heather has worked for me a long time. She's very protective. And somewhat cynical. She saw me through a very bad patch when I was confronted with the fact that a woman I'd trusted, loved, was passing insider information to her brother to play the stock market. Using me to get advance knowledge of mergers and take-overs to buy up shares that they knew would rise fast once the news became public.'

'That's serious, isn't it?'

'If I'd been implicated I could have gone to jail.'

'Did they? Go to jail.'

'No. I didn't believe it. I was so certain that I said I'd prove it, and I set a trap. A bogus take-over of a dummy company. I took a report home in my briefcase—something I'd done a hundred times before—setting out my plans to take it over.'

She didn't say anything, but he saw the question in her eyes.

'When someone started buying huge blocks of shares I confronted her. They took off—disappeared one step ahead of the police. He wasn't her brother, of course.'

'But that's…'

Words apparently failed her, but he wouldn't have been human not to feel warmed by her look of compassion. He refused to let her shift all the blame.

'She couldn't have deceived me if I'd been paying attention, Talie. I was careless. Took her apparent adoration as nothing less my due. I was, after all, the brilliant Jude Radcliffe. She saw that weakness in me and exploited it.'

'All you were guilty of was trusting someone you loved. That's when you lost the wonder, isn't it? When "the deal" became the only thing you believed in?'

'I took a ride to the top of the Empire State with you.'

'Only because you had your arm twisted. You'd seen it all before.'

'I thought I had, but I saw something new tonight,' he said.

'Oh? And what was that?'

'I'll tell you if you'll stop avoiding my question. Why can't you take on the kind of commitment that working for me would entail?'

'It's nothing,' she said, far too quickly, and for once not quite prepared to meet his eyes. 'Family commitments, that's all.'

'If it's nothing, why won't you talk about it?' he persisted.

That caught her attention, but her eyes were like those of a startled creature caught in car headlights.

She held the stare for another ten seconds before breaking free. Then, with a shrug, she said, 'We don't—Calhouns. Talk.'

He might have offered her an argument about that, but he refused to take the bait and let her off the hook. Refused to say anything that would give her another chance to run away down some other conversational back alley.

For a moment she actually looked panic stricken. Then she groaned, dropping her face into her hands, and before he could think he was on his knees in front of her, taking her hands, forcing her to look at him.

'I trusted you, Talie. Trust me. Talk to me. Tell me what's wrong.'

She shook her head. 'Nothing. It's nothing. I've just realised that I'm just like her, that's all.'

'Who?'

'My mother. That's what she used to do. She was so good at changing the subject that you wouldn't notice. Get too close and she was off, rattling away about nothing. She had it down to a fine art. And if you got a bit insistent about going out for the day, or asked wasn't it time she had a holiday, she'd divert you with some article she'd read in a magazine. She read so many magazines—'

'Talie…'

She held up one hand to stop him. 'It's okay. I'm not doing that. Just trying to explain.'

'Take your time. Here. Come on.' And he reached out, gathered her in his arm so that she slithered down beside him.

After a deep breath, she said, 'My mother isn't well, Jude. I take care of her most of the time. Every few months Karen, her younger sister, comes and gives me a break so that I get a week or two out of the house.'

He didn't understand what distressed her so much about that. Or the fact that she'd found it so hard to tell him.

'You take a temporary job?' he prompted. 'Instead of taking a holiday?'

'I don't need a holiday. I need to be in the real world for a little while. To pretend that I've got an ordinary life.'

Instead of staying at home with a sick mother, watching sentimental movies. And he felt his blood run cold as he remembered telling her that she should get out more.

CHAPTER NINE

'Is it terminal?' Jude asked.

Talie shook her head. 'No. Terminal illness is something that people understand, sympathise with. My mother has agoraphobia. And since my father died there have been bouts of depression, too. Those why-don't-you-just-snap-out-of-it syndromes that irritate people who have no idea of the reality.'

'They are illnesses every bit as real, every bit as debilitating as any other disease.'

She smiled briefly at his understanding.

'Obviously it had been there for a long time, but Liam was away on a gap year in Australia, and I'd moved in with the man I assumed in that careless way of the young was going to be the till-death-do-us-part love of my life. It was only when my dad died that we discovered how bad it was. If I'd been home more, if I'd actually listened, stopped to think, take some notice…' She looked across at him. 'But your parents are always there, aren't they? Boring, grey people who don't do much and who you never think of as having feelings. Neither of them were the sort of people to talk about feelings.'

'Do you know what triggered it?'

'Apparently she lost a baby. Her first child. She had an emergency Caesarean but he had something wrong with his heart and didn't survive. I didn't know about it until after my dad died and everything fell apart.'

'I see.'

'Do you?' She looked up at him then. 'Everything was different then—brushed under the carpet as if it had never happened. No one ever talked about it. Not family. Not friends. She never had a chance to grieve. She was just encouraged to have another baby, as if that was all she needed. As if I could ever replace the one that was lost.'

'I'm so sorry.'

She managed a smile. 'More than you wanted to know, right?'

Wrong. He wanted to know everything.

'It's okay,' she went on, before he could reassure her. 'Really. At least we don't have to worry about money. Dad had that covered. He dealt with his own grief by working so hard that he dropped dead with a massive heart attack when he was fifty-two. But then Mum wouldn't go out, or away on holiday, so what else was he to do?'

'Talie—'

He had his arm around her, but it wasn't enough. He wanted to wrap her up in his arms, hold her, tell her that he would make everything right for her.

'I was so stupid,' she said, looking up at him, her eyes clouded with a sadness that tugged at a heart he'd put into cold storage years ago. The pain he was feeling had to be the return of warmth, love… 'I never caught on. She always had some excuse not to go out, some really convincing reason why she couldn't come and visit me in the new flat *this* week. And of course I was so busy with my own life that I let her get away with it.'

'Don't—'

'I was always trying to tempt her with brochures for exotic holidays, but she used to say that she couldn't leave her garden, or that Dad was too busy. And because he didn't deny it—protecting her because she didn't want us to know that she was a prisoner in her own home—I used to blame him.'

'And now you're blaming yourself.'

'Well, it's ironic, isn't it? I'm always leaping up to help total strangers, but when my mother needed me, my father needed me—'

'It's not your fault.' He had to convince her of that. 'Look at me, Talie.' She raised her lashes and looked at him with those amazing blue eyes that had held him prisoner since she'd first looked up at him in the lift and he'd have done anything to convince her. 'There's help out there. All kinds of help—'

'There were drugs for the depression. Once we realised that she needed help. But getting her to leave the safety of the house is different. She has to want that, and until she's ready to take that step I have to be there for her. She's mentally very fragile, Jude.' She briefly covered his hand with hers, then pulled away from him, sat up. 'I know you're trying to help, but you must see that even if you wanted me to work for you it just wouldn't be possible.'

'This isn't about me, it's about you. Your mother isn't the only one who needs help.'

'You think I'm the one who needs counselling?'

He didn't know what he meant—for once in his life he felt utterly helpless.

'I think you need to stop bottling it up. And you need to get out of the house or you'll become trapped there, just like your mother.'

'No, I'm out all the time. I do the shopping. Take a run every morning.'

'On your own?' And, when she didn't deny it, 'What about the theatre? Dinner with friends? Dates? Something as simple as a trip to the cinema to see the latest movie instead of an old video at home.'

That she didn't answer was answer enough.

'Maybe you're the one who needs a twelve-step programme, angel. To get a life.'

'I guess I deserved that,' she said. 'But I still can't work for you.'

'No?' He didn't give a hoot about that, he had no intention of offering her a job, but he wasn't going to turn down any lever to prise her free. He sympathised with her mother, but his concern was for Talie. 'So, will you tell Heather that she's got to put her plans for full time grandmotherhood on hold, or shall I?'

'You'll find someone, Jude.' She caught a yawn. 'Oh, now I'm sleepy,' she said with a smile. 'Just as it's getting light.'

'It's still very early. You might manage an hour or two.'

'Yes, well, I suppose it's worth a try. Thanks for listening.'

He stood up, pulled her to her feet. 'Anytime,' he said.

She picked up their mugs, took them through to the kitchen. He heard the tap run as she rinsed them out. About to tell her to leave it, that the maid would see to it, he remembered her bed—and realised she'd made it herself. And he knew that was how she filled her days. With endless small, repetitive jobs to stop herself from going mad.

A moment or two later her door closed quietly as she returned to her room. He should try to sleep, too. But he didn't move. The only reason she'd told him about her mother, he realised, was because she'd had that momentary glimpse of reality, a sudden fear that she was becoming like her, and he was glad he'd pushed. She needed to recognise the danger.

But that wasn't why he'd done it. He'd wanted to know her, know her secrets. He'd wanted her to trust him, and she had.

So what did he do now?

Talie woke to the faint sound of traffic in the street below. Despite the yawn, she had been certain the dredging up of painful truths would have kept her awake, but she must have fallen asleep as soon as her head touched the pillow.

She checked the time. It was still early and, rolling out of bed, she dressed quickly, hoping to get out of the suite before Jude stirred, keen to avoid him after the pathetic way she'd spilled out her problems.

More than he'd wanted to know—more than any man wanted to know, as she'd discovered for herself the hard way. Unluckily for him he'd caught her in that low ebb of even the most optimistic heart, which came in the darkest hours of the night, when the tunnel seemed endless and there was no light to show a way out.

He'd have done better to have joined her in bed. That way they'd both have had a good time. For a moment when he'd opened her door, just stood there looking at her, she'd thought…hoped…

Obviously she needed a cold shower, she decided, shaking her head to rid it of such nonsense and tugging on her shorts. She hadn't been in such close quarters with a man since she'd had to choose between her mother and the man she'd been in love with.

Had never wanted to be.

Fortunately for her, in these days of sexual harassment in the workplace charges no man was going to take that kind of risk with a girl who worked for him.

Listening to her sob story had to be safer.

He was a good listener.

And he was right. It had helped to talk. She'd slipped into a dull acceptance of the situation. When she got home she would try again to get her mother to see someone. And if she wouldn't—well, she might take his advice and seek counselling herself. Someone to talk to who wasn't involved, someone detached. Maybe Jude Radcliffe would volunteer…

She pulled the lace of her running shoe so tight that it snapped.

Taking a deep breath, she concentrated on re-threading it, and when that was done she pulled her hair into a band to keep it off her face and eased open the door to the sitting room.

Jude, stripped and ready for action in cut-offs and a T-shirt, glanced pointedly at his wristwatch as he rose from the armchair. 'I was beginning to think I was going to have to come and throw cold water over you.'

Cold water. Good idea.

'Let's go,' he said.

'I'm sorry? Go where?'

'I'm taking your advice—abandoning CNN and the Dow Jones Index for fresh air.' He tossed her a bottle of water and opened the door. 'Last one to Bow Bridge buys breakfast,' he said as he summoned the lift.

She tried to think of something sensible to say. More importantly to find the breath to say it with.

'You have got to be joking.'

Oh, that was good…

'Joking? Why would you think that? I'm here—'

She shook her head as she stepped into the lift. 'Not about coming with me. About a race to the bridge. Let's face it,' she began again, attempting to make herself clear, 'your legs…'

Her mouth dried as she found herself staring at them.

'What's the matter with my legs?'

Nothing. Not one thing. They were actually just about the most perfect legs she'd ever seen on a man.

'Mmm?'

Recollecting herself, she looked up. He was regarding her intently, and she wondered how on earth she'd ever thought his eyes were like slate. They were the dark blue-grey of storm clouds, swirling with danger, but always with the promise that the sun would break through in a shower of silver light. Last night she'd seen it for herself, and she knew that the mask he wore in the office was not the true man. That he blamed himself for making a mistake, for a lapse of judgement, and had shut himself away from the risk of repeating it.

'Talie?'

'What? Oh, they're, um, very…long. They give you an unfair advantage.'

'Not from where I'm standing. To win I'd have to pass you, and deprive myself of the pleasure of looking at yours.'

He should be smiling if he was teasing…

'Should you be saying something like that to your secretary?'

'My secretary would never appear in public wearing cut-offs and a cropped T-shirt that exposes several inches of bare midriff.' And he did that thing with the eyebrow again.

Just when she was getting her breath back and her heart rate under control.

'If I'd known you were going to join me, Jude, neither would I.' Then, as the lift doors opened, she said, 'See you at the bridge.' And she took off, not even having to pause at the door, since a grinning porter leapt to open it for her. The street was quiet and she crossed it without looking back, determined to make him work to keep up with her if it killed her.

And it very nearly did.

'It looks like breakfast's on me,' he said, leaning against the parapet of the bridge as he tipped up his water bottle.

She was fit, she ran every morning, but she'd pushed herself to the limit and was bent from the waist, hands on her knees, trying to ignore the fact that he wasn't even breathing heavily.

'Rubbish,' she gasped, looking up at him. 'You could have taken me any time.'

'Why would I want to do that when I was having such a good time?'

This was definitely a moment for cold water, and she took a long draught from the bottle. She'd have tipped the rest over him, but her need was greater so she poured it over her head and face.

'Come on—you'd better keep moving.'

Obviously this was a good idea, but she didn't bother to say so, saving her breath for running, setting off at a brisk pace. She was immediately jerked back as Jude grabbed a handful of T-shirt.

'Slow down,' he said. 'Take time to enjoy the view.'

'Enjoy the view?' And she stopped, turned to him, placed her hand on his forehead before shaking her head. 'Extraordinary. I was sure you must be suffering from a fever. It must be lack of sleep. You'd better put off your take-over plans; the opposition will run rings around you in this mood.'

'I'm not going to give them the chance. Did you bring your camera today?'

Oh, right. Slow on the uptake, or what? He was feeling guilty for being so mean about sightseeing. Because she never got out of the house. This was his attempt at being *nice* to her.

'Look, if this is about last night there's absolutely no need for you—'

'Did you?'

'—to do this. I wasn't asking for your pity and I don't want it.'

'Who said anything about pity? I was simply offering you a photo opportunity,' he said.

Now she just felt stupid.

'I'm not denying that I admire your kindness, and your loyalty to your mother, Talie, but there are a lot of people in worse predicaments than you.'

Really stupid.

'Well, I'm glad we cleared that up. But, thanks, I took photographs yesterday.'

'But none of them had you in them,' he pointed out. 'Your mother would enjoy them a lot more if she could see you having a good time.'

She knew he was right, but she still left her camera undisturbed in the little bag she wore buckled around her waist. Any photographs of her would be an enduring memory of the man who'd taken them, and some memories it was wiser not to build.

'Jude, I'm here to work, as you have constantly reminded me. And I came out to run. If you want to walk back, I'll see you later.' She didn't wait for him to make a decision but set off briskly and didn't look back.

She knew he was keeping pace with her, her skin was crackling with the tension that seemed to snap between them, but even so she jumped when his hand came over her head to push the door open and hold it for her when she reached the hotel.

'Thank you.' Then, in the lift, attempting to be businesslike, 'What time do you want Barney to pick us up, Jude?'

'We don't need Barney today.'

'We don't? But—'

'I called Marcus last night and asked him to handle today's negotiations. I have something more important to do.'

'You're kidding me? What the heck could be more important than a take-over you've been planning for months?'

'A visit to the Statue of Liberty. A walk through Greenwich Village. Lunch in Little Italy. Maybe an art gallery—' He glanced at her. 'What else do you have on your list?'

'List?'

'You said the Empire State Building was at the top of your list…'

'Jude, get real. You didn't bring me to New York to go sightseeing. You've got to be there today,' she said, a touch desperately. 'It's important—'

'No. Life is important. That's just business. Marcus can handle it. So, what are we going to do first?'

'How about getting a grip on reality—?'

'That's exactly what I am doing. Besides, it's years since I've taken time out to look at the city.'

'Jude—' she began, knowing that she should protest.

He didn't look at her, just reached out and took her hand in a silencing gesture. Then, briskly, 'I'll give you twenty minutes to get ready. Wear comfortable shoes.'

'Hold it, mister!'

Confronted by this suddenly fierce little bombshell, legs astride, arms akimbo, Jude was sorely tempted to laugh. He'd felt like that a lot since Talie erupted into his life. It was the kind of feeling a man could get used to. But he managed to contain himself.

'What's the problem?'

For a moment he could see the battle between what she knew she should say and what she wanted to say going on inside her head. Then she said, 'Comfortable shoes? You are going to make me *walk* around New York?'

'Not everywhere. I thought we'd take the subway, just a couple of stops, so that you could say you've done it. We don't want to waste too much time underground when we could be on a bus seeing the sights. I might even hail a yellow cab, if you behave yourself.'

'Why? Why are you doing this for me?'

He could have told her then. The temptation was there. But it wasn't the right time. It was too soon. She wouldn't believe he was serious. He could hardly believe it himself.

'For you? This isn't for you, Talie Calhoun. This is for me. Step one on that twelve-step programme you advocated, remember? I'm searching for my sense of wonder,' he said.

This wasn't entirely true. His sense of wonder might have been hibernating, buried under a pile of paper, hiding away behind the barrier of an abrupt, repelling manner from any risk that it might take another beating—a barrier that had crumpled when Talie Calhoun bounded into his lift a couple of weeks ago—but it was wide awake now, and hungry.

'As my secretary, it's your duty to help me find it.'

She didn't move.

'In return I'll show you the city. I'll even take photographs of you having lunch, if you like.'

'Twenty minutes?'

'Fifteen, now. You've wasted five of them talking.'

CHAPTER TEN

THEY began by squashing into a subway train full of office workers heading downtown. Jude had intended to get off after a couple of stops, but he was enjoying the excuse to put his arm around her, protect her with his body from the crush too much to surrender it, and they stayed on until they were forced to change at Washington Square, where they stopped for breakfast.

'This is Greenwich Village, right?'

'Right,' he confirmed. 'You have a movie memory you want to share?'

'I don't spend my entire life watching movies.' And, before he could ask her what she did do, she jumped in with, 'What about you? I know a multimillionaire's work is never done, but there must be more to life than—'

'Money?'

'Work.'

'I keep busy.' She grinned. 'What?' She shook her head. 'No, come on. If you've got something to say, spit it out.'

'It just occurred to me that we're as sad as one another. You're so caught up in business that you've stopped seeing anything beyond the end of your desk. I'm caught up in my poor mother's fear of the outside world. We don't have a life between us.'

'I'd already worked that out for myself. That's why we're sitting here over a leisurely breakfast overlooking the park, instead of closeted in a lawyer's office.'

'Well. Good.'

'Very good.'

They took a bus the rest of the way to Battery Park, bought tickets for the boat, and stood at the stern watching the Manhattan skyline retreat as they headed for Liberty Island. They bought a guidebook and walked around the statue, informing each other of the more amazing statistics until rain forced them to dive for cover in the gift shop.

Talie picked out a postcard to send to her brother, some keyrings to give to neighbours, then, spotting some green foam sponge 'Liberty' ray headbands, she said, 'Oh, my gosh, I have to have one of those for my god-daughter.'

'God-daughter? You have a god-daughter?'

'I'm getting to an age where my friends have children.' She grinned. 'Some of them are even thinking of getting married.'

'What happened to the till-death-do-us-part guy?' Jude asked.

And this time there was no hesitation, no change-the-subject conversational sidestep. 'Mark didn't bargain on my mother being part of the package.'

'Terrific.'

'It's okay. I didn't like his mother either.' Then, because he didn't say anything, 'No, you're right, Jude. It wasn't okay. It hurt like hell. But what was I going to do?'

'There's been no one else since?' Her turn to be silent. 'Just because your mother doesn't go out, it doesn't mean you can't, Talie.'

'No, but she always has to come first. Men can't deal with that.' She looked out. 'I think it's stopped raining.'

'Great. Time for one more photograph before we move on.' And he fitted the 'ray' headdress around her curls and handed her a bottle of cola. 'Hold that up.'

'I can't!'

'That little kid over there is doing it.'

'He's five years old!' But she did it anyway, because she wanted to see him grin again, to forget for a moment that it was just…a moment in time. That tomorrow they would fly home and her adventure would be over. 'I can't believe I let you talk me into that,' she said, as they walked back to the boat.

'It'll make your mother laugh.'

'Yes, it will. Thank you.'

Jude stuck his arm out for her to hook hers around it. 'Okay—next stop, Ellis Island.'

They stayed longer than they'd meant to, looking at the piles of luggage, the photographs. Reading the names. Listening to the echoes of history.

'Hungry?' he asked, as they boarded the boat back to Manhattan. She nodded. 'Italian, Chinese…?'

'American. A deli sandwich. I have to have pastrami on rye.'

'You do?'

'It's on the list,' she said, looking up with something that started as a grin but faded into something intense, unreadable, and Jude felt such a jolt of longing that it almost took his breath away. In the midst of the crowded, noisy boat they were for a moment locked in a bubble of silence. A place where words were redundant. A place where no one could intrude.

He reached up, touched her cheek with his knuckles, and then, when she didn't pull away, opened his hand and laid his palm against its softness.

She swayed into him as the boat began to move, and he put his hand to her waist to steady her. Holding her close. Asking all kinds of questions with his eyes, his hands, his body.

Then a child stumbled over a bag and fell at her feet and any answers were blown away.

Or maybe the speed with which she moved to pick up the boy, smile at him before he could even think of crying, was all the answer he needed.

'I'm so sorry,' his mother apologised to both of them, as if aware that her son had broken into a charmed moment.

'Don't be,' Jude said. 'He's a lovely boy.' He turned to lean on the rail. 'We're nearly there,' he said, glancing sideways at Talie.

'Yes.'

Nearly. But she would need time. It was okay. There was no rush. Talie was special. Well worth waiting for. And as they left the park he hailed a yellow cab, and took a photograph of her getting into it before telling the driver to take them to Katz's Deli for pastrami on whatever kind of bread she wanted.

They didn't speak on the way there, but the cab driver filled the silence with a running commentary on the sights they passed, on the mayor, on the impossibility of the traffic. And when Jude took her hand she didn't pull away.

But when they had their food and were settled at a table she was still unnaturally quiet, picking at her food instead of tucking in. He said, 'Is there a problem?' She glanced at him. 'You're quiet. Is sightseeing losing it's thrill? Or is it me?'

'You?' She smiled. 'No, Jude. You've been great.' And she said it with sufficient conviction to give him the kind of warm, fuzzy feeling that he'd been avoiding for so long. 'Sorry. I was miles away. What did you want to talk about?'

'Nothing. Silence is good.'

'A relief, I should think. I know I talk too much. I engage complete strangers in conversation at the bus stop or the supermarket checkout, given the slightest encouragement.'

'You even talk to strange men in lifts.'

She grinned. 'I'm incorrigible.'

'I'm glad. If you hadn't talked to me I wouldn't have told Heather about you, and she wouldn't have checked you out and chosen you to come to New York.'

'And you'd be sitting in a boring meeting instead of having lunch with me.'

He doubted the meeting was boring, but he was content with the choice he'd made. More than content.

'So, how are you feeling? On the wonder scale?' she asked brightly, making a determined effort to shake off whatever melancholy dogged her.

'Is that between one and ten?'

'There is nothing so cut and dried about wonder, Jude. It goes to infinity and beyond.'

'Does it? I thought that was Superman.'

'Actually, it's Buzz Lightyear,' she admitted. '*Toy Story* and *Toy Story 2*. Great movies…' She stopped. 'I'll eat my lunch now.'

But he caught her hand as she reached for the fork. 'The answer to your question is infinity,' he said.

For a moment she looked confused. Then she blushed.

And then he knew, without doubt, that he was in love. He knew that because what he felt was more than an urgent and over-whelming desire to possess her. To make love to her. It was a desire to protect her. To cherish her. To know that he could tease her and have her look at him like that fifty years from now.

What he said was, 'So, what do you want to do this afternoon? An art gallery, Radio City, the Metropolitan Museum of Art?'

'It's too nice to be indoors.'

'We could take a boat out on the lake in Central Park. Ride on the carousel. Or just lie on the grass, eating ice cream and looking at the sky.' Then, 'Or all of the above.'

'Hey, I'm impressed. You catch on fast.'

'You can't go home without eating ice cream. It's a national institution.'

'You won't get an argument from me.'

'Then I'll take that as a yes. But first we have to choose a gift for Heather's granddaughter. Any ideas?'

'Well, silver is traditional. A baby bracelet?'

'If you wanted to take a look around Tiffany's you just had to say so, Talie. Just don't ask for breakfast.'

'I really would like to take a look around Tiffany's,' she said.

Her reward for admitting it was a silver key-ring with a red enamelled apple fob. It came in its own turquoise suede drawstring bag, which was put inside a turquoise box, which was put inside a little turquoise carrier bag with 'Tiffany & Co' in discreet black lettering.

'I feel like Audrey Hepburn,' Talie said, as Jude handed the bag to her. 'Apart from the hair, obviously—'

'I love your hair. Every ridiculous curl of it,' he interrupted, sparking a dangerous warmth that spread from the vicinity of her waist to leave her feeling oddly weak at the knees. He caught her arm as they buckled.

'—and the little black dress,' she finished.

'You've got a little black dress,' he said, and his voice wasn't entirely steady either, she noticed.

'So I have.' She'd known that dress was special the moment she'd slipped it over her head. She'd been disappointed with his first reaction to it, but it had got her to the top of the Empire State Building. A dress that could do that—

'Wear it this evening and we'll round off the evening with dinner somewhere very special.'

* * *

They spent the afternoon in the park, laughing and talking. Not about movies, or business, but about themselves. Pretending for a few hours that anything was possible. And later Barney drove them across the Brooklyn Bridge to a floating restaurant, where they had dinner with all the lights of Manhattan shining in the darkness.

'It's been a lovely day, Jude. I'll never forget it,' Talie said.

He reached across the table, took her hand. 'It's not quite over. There's one more thing we have to do.'

'Jude—' she began, but her voice broke on his name.

'A buggy ride?' he said. 'For two?'

After a day in which they'd seemed never to stopped talking they were finally silent, with only the clipping sound of the horse's hooves as she took her own sweet time on her stately ride around the park.

It wasn't an awkward silence, but the quiet that came at the end of a perfect day, when you had your arm around the woman you were falling in love with, her head tucked against your shoulder, the scent of her hair, her skin, stealing your mind.

'Talie?'

She lifted her head from his shoulder to look up at him.

'On that wonder scale of yours…I've just decided that infinity is nowhere near high enough to describe the day I've had. I'm upgrading my assessment to "beyond."'

She smiled. 'But that doesn't leave you with anywhere to go. It's like saying it can't get any better than this.'

'You're telling me it can?'

Talie understood what he was asking, but last night's fantasy thoughts about him climbing into bed with her and them both having a good time with no strings attached had been just that. A fantasy. She wanted it every bit as much as he did, but she wasn't built that way. So, instead of the invitation to show him how much better it could be that he undoubtedly expected, she said, 'You have to believe that or what's the point?'

He took her hand, raised it to his lips and kissed it. 'I believe,' he said. And then, cradling her cheek in the palm of his hand, he bent to kiss her.

He didn't rush at it. Well, she knew the measure of the man.

She'd spent three days with him. Watched him working. Heard him talking to his staff, his peers. He knew how to plan, knew not to barge in and take what he wanted, but to make surrender seem like a victory.

As he touched his lips to the delicate skin at her temple she discovered that she'd been holding her breath, waiting, wanting this… He moved to her eyelids, touching each of them with butterfly-soft kisses, and she heard herself utter a little give-away sigh. He brushed her cheek, lingered at the spot where a dimple refused to accept that she was grown up and go away. And then his lips touched her mouth with the gentlest of kisses, asking, *Do you want this? Is this too much? Show me…*

Not only did she want it, Talie knew that this was the kiss she'd been waiting for all her life.

Perfect. Pure. Beyond.

And that was why she pulled back. Not because she didn't want to spend the night with him. But because she wanted it too much.

'Jude—'

'Shhh.' He touched her cheek with his fingers, then said, 'It's over.'

For a moment she thought he was talking about them, and felt the sharpest stab of pain. Maybe he was, or maybe he just meant that the buggy had come to a stop. But she shivered anyway as he climbed down from the buggy, feeling chilled without his warmth at her side. Then he turned and held out his hand to help her down, tucking her arm under his as they crossed the road to the hotel, where they rode in silence up to their suite.

'Jude—' She tried again to explain.

But he slipped the key through the lock and pushed open the door. 'Goodnight, Talie. Sleep well.'

She paused on the threshold, wanting to tell him how much the day had meant to her, how much she wished she could respond to the demands of her body, the desperate urging of her heart to show him just how much he meant to her in the only way a woman truly could.

'Don't,' he said sharply. Then, more gently, 'I'll see you in the morning.'

She stood under the shower, the first cold one of her entire life, running it until her teeth chattered. Then she pulled on the baggy T-shirt she slept in, huddled up under the covers and, with the prospect of sleep about as likely as icicles in hell, switched on the television and surfed through the channels, looking for a movie…

Jude didn't hang about in the hope that she'd change her mind. He didn't want her to change her mind. He wanted her so sure, so certain, that nothing would stop her…

He stripped off and stood under the shower until he was numb with cold. It made no difference. One kiss. He'd allowed himself one kiss, and now he was burning up, throbbing for a woman in a way he hadn't in years. But not just for any woman. Only Talie would answer his need, and she'd wanted it, too.

He'd seen it in her eyes, liquid and dark. Felt it in the way her body had softened against him as he'd kissed her. Heard it in her voice, the soft sigh, the unconscious groan of frustration as she'd pulled away from the temptation he'd offered. But she respected herself too much to take easy pleasure for one night. And why would she imagine it would be anything more?

But it wasn't just for a night.

They'd spent the afternoon talking about the past. The events that had moulded them, made them what they were. She knew more about him than even his own mother, because that was how it was when you met someone you wanted to spend the rest of your life with. She'd changed his world, changed him, and he had to tell her. She had to know…

He threw on a robe, wrenching open the door, and like some kind of miracle she was there, standing in her bedroom doorway. Hair damp, kangaroo T-shirt on inside out…

'You didn't tell me,' she said. 'You said you saw something new. Last night, when we were at the top of the Empire State Building. You said you'd tell me if I stopped avoiding your question…'

'I saw the city as I'd never seen it before. Reflected in your eyes. Turned 'round. Like my life.' He reached out a hand to her. 'Tell me what you dream about, Talie—*"when the full moon is shining in…and the lamp is dying out…"*'

'A moment like this,' she said, grasping his hand. Holding it. 'A moment of pure magic.'

'You're cold,' he said.

'Warm me.' He held her then. Put his arms around her as he'd longed to do all week and held her close, and she said, 'Love me, Jude. Just for tonight, make all my dreams come true.'

Dreams don't come true without a lot of hard work. Nothing important, truly life-changing, is ever achieved without effort.

'Stand still, Talie. These buttons are so small.'

She *was* standing still; it was her mother's fingers that were shaking, and they both knew that. But one by one the buttons were fastened, and then she slipped into the loose-fitting ivory velvet coat.

'Lovely, dear. You look absolutely lovely.'

'And so do you.'

Her mother was wearing a coat and hat in a heavy deep blue silk that matched her eyes. Not that you could see much of her face. The hat was huge. It was still difficult for her to go out without somewhere to hide, to cut out the threatening spaces when she felt overwhelmed by them. But she'd been given a goal—a big enough reason to confront her fears, seek help. A reason to step outside the boundaries of her house, the safety of the walled garden at the rear.

Jude had been brilliant. Patient beyond words. Never pushing her. But never letting her slip back either. He'd sit and watch old movies with her, but afterwards he'd insist on walking her around the garden, always knowledgeably suggesting some new shrub that would do well and she should look at when she felt like a visit to the garden centre. Considering he lived in a riverside apartment, with nothing more horticulturally challenging than a balcony, he must have put in some serious homework on that front.

In fact, Jude could do no wrong in her mother's eyes.

Talie had tried to get her mother interested in joining a support group on the internet, but he'd bought her a computer of her own and signed her up to a group for people with similar problems. Not just agoraphobia, but women who'd had stillborn babies. People who could offer help in taking the small steps back into life. People who'd been there and could say with confidence, 'You can do it.' Because they'd done it themselves.

And, because Jude had done it, her mother had made the effort.

He'd talked to her about the wedding, too. Never letting her forget that it was going to happen. Involving her in plans for the service. Asking her to choose hymns. Seeking her advice about flowers.

Not that Talie had said she'd marry him. In fact she'd turned him down flat. But of course he just wouldn't take no for an answer. He'd treated the problem exactly like any other take-over bid, and had had no intention of letting go until he had got what he wanted.

And how could you fight a man like that?

A man who came to see you every day, no matter how busy he was, no matter how often you told him to stay away.

Who held your mother's hand as he coaxed her down a canvas tunnel he'd had erected from the front door to the gate and into the rear of a car with specially tinted windows and took them both to see the newest chick-flick.

Who bought a house with a wing for your mother and then asked her to help him find the perfect housekeeper. Someone who would always be there.

Who conspired with your mother and your aunt to whisk you off to New York for a long weekend, refusing to leave Tiffany's until you'd chosen not only an engagement ring, but a wedding ring, too.

Who could resist such a man?

He knew how to plan, knew how to take his time, knew how to make surrender seem like a victory. And, sooner rather than later, her mother had surrendered and promised that on her wedding day she would give her daughter away.

The tunnel to the gate was no longer a temporary canvas shield but a delicately arched pergola, that would one day be dripping with wisteria, but for her wedding day it was woven with winter evergreens, bright berries, and ribbons that matched the pretty tartan dresses of her bridesmaids.

And if it was her brother, Liam, and Talie who supported their mother to the car, rather than the other way around, that was okay. She was getting there. Stronger day by day.

Jude turned and stood even before the vicar had given the signal—before the organist began to play, before Talie started towards him, a vision in a softly draped full-length coat of ivory velvet, open over a simple matching dress. Her hair, her lovely hair, was threaded with ivy and berries and tiny roses, her eyes a pure, true blue.

And as she walked on her mother's arm towards him those eyes never left him, until her mother placed her hand in his and took a step back.

'Dearly beloved…' the vicar began, and Jude closed his fingers over hers so that she knew he would never let her go as they turned together to face the future as a family.

There are 24 timeless classics in the Mills & Boon® 100th Birthday Collection

Two of these beautiful stories are out each month. Make sure you collect them all!

If you have missed any of these books, log on to www.millsandboon.co.uk to order your copies online.